"SOMETIMES," JACK SAID QUIETLY, "ALL WE CAN DO is trust the things we don't understand."

"I'm not sure that I can," Chloe said.

Her voice was so low and alluring that he ached, heart and soul, with longing to possess this woman. "I won't rush you." He meant his promise.

"I won't be rushed," she confirmed before her gaze fell to his lips. She exhaled unsteadily.

His heart raced. He tried not to overreact to the invitation in the sound. "Will you try to trust whatever happens between us?"

"Why?" she asked softly.

"Because I think it might be very important."

"Jack . . ." she began, worry evident in her tone.

"Please don't, Chloe."

With that plea voiced, he lowered his head and blocked out the pale winter sun. He claimed her lips as she whispered his name. And in that simple act, he claimed Chloe McNeil. Gently. Thoroughly. Inexorably.

WHAT ARE *LOVESWEPT* ROMANCES?

They are stories of true romance and touching emotion. We believe those two very important ingredients are constants in our highly sensual and very believable stories in the LOVE-SWEPT line. Our goal is to give you, the reader, stories of consistently high quality that may sometimes make you laugh, sometimes make you cry, but are always fresh and creative and contain many delightful surprises within their pages.

Most romance fans read an enormous number of books. Those they truly love, they keep. Others may be traded with friends and soon forgotten. We hope that each LOVESWEPT romance will be a treasure—a "keeper." We will always try to publish

LOVE STORIES YOU'LL NEVER FORGET
BY AUTHORS YOU'LL ALWAYS REMEMBER

The Editors

Loveswept 863

THE CHRISTMAS GIFT

LAURA TAYLOR

BANTAM BOOKS
NEW YORK · TORONTO · LONDON · SYDNEY · AUCKLAND

THE CHRISTMAS GIFT
A Bantam Book / December 1997

ISBN 0-553-44603-7

Published simultaneously in the United States and Canada

Bantam Books are published by Bantam Books, a division of Bantam Dou-
bleday Dell Publishing Group, Inc. Its trademark, consisting of the words
"Bantam Books" and the portrayal of a rooster, is Registered in U.S.
Patent and Trademark Office and in other countries. Marca Registrada.
Bantam Books, 1540 Broadway, New York, New York 10036.

PRINTED IN THE UNITED STATES OF AMERICA
OPM   10 9 8 7 6 5 4 3 2 1

Merry Christmas to
Kathie, Jeff, Kaitlin,
and Taylor Antrim.
With love,
LT

ONE

Jack Howell stood at the edge of the crowd. He felt remarkably at ease, and he savored the feeling as he half listened to snippets of conversation and gentle bursts of laughter from the clusters of people around him.

After handing his empty champagne flute to a passing waiter, he began to thread his way through the crush of guests. Jack nodded in greeting to several people he'd met since arriving in the area four months earlier, but he didn't linger to chat. Although he was enjoying the afternoon's festivities, he wanted a few quiet moments to himself.

The instincts of a lifetime, instincts rooted in childhood and developed to razor-sharp precision as an adult, assured him that he had nothing to be wary about among this group. Having spent his youth at the mercy of others and the twenty years since college and law school as a senior investigator and attorney for the Justice Department, Jack trusted his instincts.

Friends, coworkers, and adversaries alike realized that Jack Howell was a man who knew, understood, and accepted himself. He possessed the unflinching nature and intellect of a skilled hunter and the tactical abilities of a chess master. He was something of a loner, less by design than by the circumstances supplied by that unpredictable entity called fate.

The guests gathered to celebrate the christening of Viva and Spence Hammond's first child served to remind Jack yet again of both his past and the new path he now walked. His was a journey of choice and optimism, despite forty-four years of dealing with the disappointment that was part and parcel of the human condition. It wasn't his style to whine when things didn't go his way. Instead, he moved forward, often into the unknown, with courage and steadiness.

In his heart Jack had always longed for a different kind of life, the kind that didn't involve the pursuit of deadly felons, although one such creature had unexpectedly led him to the discovery of his birth father, Tommy Conrad. He didn't know quite how to define a normal life, so he refrained from assuming that he would ever have one. But he desired a simpler way of doing and thinking and living.

As he slowly navigated the crowd Jack was amazed by the hospitality he'd already experienced from the rural Kentucky community devoted almost exclusively to the breeding and racing of some of the finest Thoroughbred horse stock in the world. Although his birth father had passed away a few years before, Jack had wanted to explore the roots of the man who'd fathered him.

Tommy Conrad. His birth father. Entrepreneur, humanitarian, advocate for the less advantaged, and guardian to his cousin following the loss of her parents during her childhood. Tommy Conrad had been a man for all seasons. Jack appreciated the time they'd had together, although he regretted that they hadn't had the traditional father-and-son relationship that many people take for granted. In private moments he consoled himself with the fact that he and Tommy had enjoyed a few years of friendship, mutual respect, and a common cause.

Jack knew that everyone assembled at the christening had considered Tommy their friend and a force in the Thoroughbred world. And because of his connection to Tommy Conrad, he had been, and continued to be, accepted by them.

Jack smiled when he caught his cousin's eye and saw her wide grin. He owed Viva a great deal, starting with her willingness to set herself up as a decoy in a dangerous cat-and-mouse game that had culminated in the capture of one Daltry Renaud, and followed by her open-armed acceptance of her late uncle's illegitimate son. He thought of Viva, her husband, and their newborn daughter as his family, and he deeply valued the relationship, having never experienced a sense of really belonging until now.

Jack finally exited the crowded formal living

room. Familiar with the layout of the mansion, he strolled down the hallway that led to the kitchen. He paused in the doorway when he spotted Chloe Mc-Neil, whom he'd met at the start of the afternoon.

Looking up from the platter she'd just placed on the kitchen counter, she smiled. As he met her smile with one of his own, Jack again sensed the strength of character he'd noticed in her earlier.

He guessed her to be in her mid-thirties. Her Irish heritage was evident in her huge green eyes, fair complexion, rosy cheeks, and the cloud of reddish-gold waves that framed her heart-shaped face.

Clad in a black pin-striped coatdress, dark hosiery, and high-heeled pumps, with gold jewelry at her ears and throat, she looked elegant. Chloe McNeil wasn't classically beautiful. Striking was a better word for her, Jack decided as he walked into the center of the sprawling kitchen. Very striking. And far more sensual than she seemed to realize.

"Mr. Howell, are you enjoying yourself?" she asked.

"Very much, thank you, but please call me Jack."

"And I'm Chloe," she added. "How are you adjusting to life in Kentucky?"

He smiled. "So far, I haven't got any complaints."

"It's quite different from Washington."

"True, but then I imagine leaving Boston was a challenge for you, as well."

She laughed at the ease with which he'd pinpointed her accent. "You're very good."

"I traveled a lot during my years at Justice. Do you get back to the East Coast very often?"

"Not as often as my brothers and sisters would like," she answered. She regarded him with a speculative expression. "Are you starting to feel less like an outsider?"

Jack didn't try to sidestep her question. If anything, he respected her directness. "To some degree. Did you have a hard time at first?"

She nodded. "For a while. I was a dedicated city dweller when I arrived ten years ago, so it took me a little longer than most. If you give yourself time to become a part of the community, you won't regret it."

"Everyone's been very gracious."

Her green eyes danced with amusement. "And very curious, I would imagine. Although most people won't pry unless you give them an opening."

"Good call," he said. "I understand why, of course."

"The announcement after Tommy's death that he had a son shocked a lot of people. Most people here are fairly nonjudgmental, though, despite the reputation that small towns tend to have for being hotbeds of gossip."

He nodded as she spoke, crossing the spacious kitchen to stand before the wall of windows. He loosened the knot of his gray-and-navy-striped tie and freed the buttons of his dark gray suit jacket as he gazed out across the seemingly endless acreage.

He scanned the surrounding landscape, noting that the lush green lawn was now snow-dusted in spots thanks to a late-November storm that had moved through the area the previous night. "I can feel their curiosity," he admitted as Chloe joined him and he turned to face her. Her fragrance, a subtle scent that reminded him of spiced vanilla, teased his senses and heightened his awareness of her on a purely physical level. "But no one's been intrusive or rude."

"You won't feel like an outsider once you've moved into your home. You'll receive invitations to join one of the local churches, and then the matchmakers will start trying to pair you up with some of the single women in the area."

Jack chuckled. "I hadn't thought of that, but I suppose I'm fair game as a bachelor."

"Well, prepare yourself," she cautioned lightly, "because the married ladies in this community are dedicated to their cause."

"Sounds like you've been the object of their good intentions."

Her expression rueful, she nodded. "A year or so after my husband died they finally gave up on me. I'm probably going to go down in local matchmaking lore as one of their few failures."

"You sound quite pleased with yourself."

"Actually, I am. I don't like being"—she paused, clearly searching for the appropriate word—"managed, even when people mean well. I've been on my own for almost five years now."

"And you like your independence," he speculated.

"I won't deny the obvious."

"It has its advantages, but only up to a point," he finished quietly. "Even busy people experience loneliness."

"So do married people," she reminded him, a hint of sadness in her green eyes before she blinked it away. Chloe exhaled softly, then asked, "How's the restoration coming along?"

Jack didn't resist her effort to shift the conversation to less personal matters, although he was more intrigued by what Chloe McNeil *hadn't* said. In her case, vagueness spoke volumes, and he sensed that her marriage hadn't been the happiest time of her life.

She gave him a curious look as his silence persisted. "The restoration?" she prodded ever so gently.

"The restoration's on track. My contractor expects to be done by midweek," he answered, not really surprised that she knew he'd spent the last four months overseeing the rehabilitation of his birth father's first home, an estate known locally as Fairhaven.

"Are you happy with Don's work?" she asked, referring to the contractor he'd employed after consulting with his cousin and her husband.

"Yes." He suddenly wondered if the two were

related. They shared the same last name. "Don and his crew were able to restore all of the woodwork, which had been neglected by the various tenants who'd leased the house over the last twenty years."

"I've seen the interior of the mansion several times. The structure is sound, but the house definitely needed a complete makeover and modernizing. It's actually a fabulous house. More than a hundred years old and filled with the kind of craftsmanship you don't often see in newer homes. It reminds of some of the old Federal-style mansions in Pennsylvania and upstate New York. I think my favorite room is the library."

"Mine too," he said, charmed by her obvious enthusiasm. "I decided to expand it by paring down the size of the formal living room. Of course, Don had to start with roofing repairs and then work his way down to the basement, since nearly everything needed refurbishing, but I'm very happy with the end result."

"Definitely a challenge, but well worth the effort."

"I gather you've done this type of thing a few times."

Chloe nodded as she made her way back to a section of kitchen counter that was covered with unused crystal plates, serving bowls, and platters. "I've restored two properties in the last four years, and I've really enjoyed the process, although they always have the potential of turning into bottomless money pits if you don't have the right contractor on the job."

Jack joined her, intervening when she reached for a tall stack of crystal dishes. "Where do you want them?"

"Up there," she answered as she gestured in the direction of a nearby cupboard.

After Chloe pulled open the door, Jack placed the dishes on an empty shelf, then eased the door shut. Standing so close to her, he couldn't help inhaling the delicate fragrance she wore.

"Thank you."

"Anything else?" he asked, glancing at the other items on the counter.

"Not right now." Her smile fading, she retraced her steps to the windows.

Jack saw and felt the change in her demeanor. He sensed a tension in her that hadn't been there a few seconds earlier. He remained standing by the cupboard, his instincts cautioning him not to crowd her. "Am I keeping you from things you need to do?"

She looked momentarily startled as she met his gaze. "No."

"Is something wrong?"

She paled. "Why would you think that?"

Jack tucked his hands into the pockets of his trousers. "Just a feeling."

"It's been a hectic day. I guess I'm a little tired, that's all."

More vagueness. It disappointed him, although he kept his reaction to himself because he wasn't at all sure how to deal with it. His sensitivity to others, even the most minor changes in posture and tone of voice, was legend among his peers at Justice, but it felt profoundly more acute with Chloe McNeil.

"Don was my father-in-law," she said a few minutes later, answering the question Jack hadn't had a chance to ask.

Jack approached her slowly. "He's a nice guy."

Chloe managed a ghost of a smile. "You're right. We've become good friends over the years, and he often handles work for my clients." She hesitated briefly, then said, "He's promised me a tour of the restoration, if you don't object."

"You're an interior decorator, aren't you?" Jack asked.

Chloe laughed as she glanced at the catering supplies and food-laden trays that still littered the countertops in the spacious kitchen. "That's my day job."

Pleased that her mood had lightened, Jack relaxed and enjoyed the moment. "When you're not overseeing catered events for good friends?"

"Exactly," she clarified with a smile. "Viva and I went to school together in Boston. She's a wonderful hostess, but she has her hands full with the new baby, so I was happy to supervise for her." Her smile widened. "I have this theory that variety is the spice of life. It's not an original concept, but it works for me."

"Makes sense," Jack responded. "Keeps you from getting bored."

She laughed. "As fluffy-headed as that probably makes me sound."

"That's the last label I'd apply to you," he countered. "You strike me as the kind of person who enjoys new challenges."

"Precisely."

"About the tour," he began.

"Yes?"

He saw the sparkle of anticipation in her bright green eyes, and a surge of warmth filtered into his bloodstream as he watched her animated features. "You're welcome to stop by anytime. If I'm handy, I'll show you around myself."

"Thank you. I'm looking forward to seeing what's been accomplished at Fairhaven."

"I'll also give Don the go-ahead when I see him tomorrow. That way, you've got carte blanche whenever it's convenient for you."

"That would be lovely."

She met his gaze, and he wondered during the brief silence that followed what she saw when she looked at him. What he saw when he looked at her made his pulse speed up, and it made him aware that he wasn't immune to the kind of desire that sends heat spilling into the veins and causes it to pool in certain parts of a man's anatomy. He controlled his response to her, of course. He was too much of a gentleman not to.

"I'm getting the distinct impression that you're an unusual woman, Chloe McNeil."

Looking slightly off balance, she drew in a breath of air, then slowly released it. Jack waited for her to speak. He knew he hadn't offended her, but he felt certain that he'd surprised her.

His gaze fell to the pulse beating in the hollow of her throat, and he fought the urge to place a fingertip against it. He wanted to feel the warmth of her skin and measure the cadence of her pulse beats. He resisted even more earthy urges, wondering if he'd had too much champagne. Known for his control over himself and his environment, Jack felt oddly out of control. He wasn't altogether sure that he liked the feeling.

"Thank you. Again," she said, sounding breathless. Enticingly breathless.

He smiled as he experienced a kind of tenderness for her that gave him pause and sent a tremor of shock through his soul. "You're welcome."

"Will your furniture arrive soon?"

Furniture? He gave her a blank look. Get your mind back to the here and now, he silently told himself. "The delivery is scheduled for next week, but it's mostly cartons filled with books and some personal items."

Chloe gave him a curious look. "No furniture?"

He shrugged. "Nothing worth mentioning. I've traveled light over the years, living in furnished apartments or condominiums in buildings that supplied a domestic staff."

She winced. "I've always needed to feel rooted."

"That's kind of why I'm here," he said, surprised to hear himself admit to Chloe McNeil that he'd grown tired of his tumbleweed existence.

"Your life's going to be quite different from now on, isn't it?"

Jack didn't answer her right away. Transiency had always bee his way of life. He'd traded foster homes for the navy, followed by college, law school, and then the Justice Department. His personal relationships had followed the same track. Transient. Convenient. And without commitment. He'd never married, rationalizing during his years at Justice that he didn't have the time to search for the right partner. He knew now, of course, that he'd been lying to himself. His reticence had had more complex causes, causes he'd finally dealt with in recent years.

"You don't believe me?" she asked.

"I've always wanted a real home."

Reaching out, she lightly rested her fingertips on his forearm. "You've come to the right place, Jack Howell."

He felt simultaneously encompassed and seduced by the gentle sound of her voice. As he searched her features he saw nothing even remotely resembling pity, just compassion and understanding. Although warmed by what he saw, Jack felt a sudden twinge of awkwardness that he'd been so candid.

Chloe didn't look away, although Jack suspected that she was far more reserved and circumspect in her dealings with most men.

Something was happening between them, he realized, something that couldn't be measured or quantified. At least not yet, anyway. Jack felt compelled to trust it, whatever it was, and to explore it, but with great care and caution. As he looked at Chloe he glimpsed both confusion and an expression of shocked recognition in her eyes. He hoped that she felt a corresponding impulse to trust and to explore whatever might be happening between them.

As the moments stretched into minutes and they continued to stare at each other, Jack couldn't help thinking that they were forging one of those rare connections that happens between a man and a woman. Stunned by that possibility, he listened to his heartbeat roar in his ears, roar to the point that it almost deafened him.

"Miss McNeil?"

The spell that held them in thrall shattered like the finest crystal hurled against a stone floor. Jack flinched and shifted his attention to the woman entering the kitchen. He recognized her immediately, but he didn't completely relax. The tension tightening his body receded by degrees.

Exhaling raggedly, Chloe withdrew her hand from Jack's arm and turned away from him. "Yes, Marie?"

"Miss Viva said to remind you that you're not supposed to spend the whole afternoon working."

Jack watched the maid place an empty crystal tray on the kitchen counter and retrieve one that had already been filled with shrimp-and-mushroom-stuffed canapés.

Chloe smiled. "Please reassure her that I'm enjoying myself."

The woman cast a speculative glance at Jack, then nodded brusquely. "Yes, ma'am." She then bustled out of the kitchen.

Jack shook his head in amusement. "Every time I see Marie, I think of a drill instructor I once knew."

Laughing, Chloe glanced up at him. "She's married to one."

"I believe it."

Her laughter disappeared, along with her smile. "And what else do you believe, Jack Howell?" Chloe studied him with an intensity he now recognized as an integral part of her personality.

He didn't answer her immediately, however. He sensed that she wanted a real answer, not some careless quip. And what he wanted to do was to give Chloe a real answer, the kind of answer that would provide her with a tangible clue about what he was like as a man. He knew anything else would disappoint her. In turn, he would be disappointed, because he felt confident that she would distance herself from him as quickly as she could manage the task if he said anything that didn't ring true to her.

Jack silently vowed never to underestimate her. She was a woman of depth, intelligence, and perception. As a result, he offered her the truth.

"What I believe, Chloe McNeil, is that I'm here

to find the parts of myself that are missing. If I don't succeed, then my life will be incomplete."

Her vivid green eyes went wide with shock.

Jack didn't move a muscle. He simply watched in silence as her shock gave way to comprehension, the kind of comprehension that bares the soul and resonates within the heart.

After drawing in a steadying breath, Chloe slowly nodded. "I think I understand what you mean."

In the silence that followed, Jack saw in her expression what he felt right down to the marrow of his bones. He saw both anxiety and relief, but he wasn't able to discern which was dominant.

Chloe looked past him in the next heartbeat, and he felt a surge of protectiveness that made him want to draw her into the safety of his arms. He quelled the urge when he turned and discovered the cause of her uneasiness.

A radiant Viva, her baby daughter cradled in her arms, stood in the kitchen doorway. She grinned as she peered at Jack and Chloe. "What are you two up to?" she asked as she approached them.

"We're attempting to solve some of the world's more pressing problems," Jack quipped.

"Any luck?" Viva asked as her gaze traveled speculatively between the two.

"More discussion is warranted," Jack confided in a mock-serious tone.

Chloe nodded solemnly, although her eyes sparkled with mischief.

"This is supposed to be a party," Viva chided with a laugh. "And you're supposed to be having fun."

"I am," Chloe insisted.

"Ditto, Miss Hostess, so quit worrying."

"Now you sound like Spence. He thinks I'm a control freak."

Jack glanced at Chloe, who was shaking her head and smiling at her longtime friend.

He nodded. "I'm afraid he's right, cousin."

Viva ruefully eyed them both. "I know, but I refuse to admit that fact to the man. He's got a big enough ego as it is." She looked down at the infant sleeping in her arms, then confessed in a soft voice, "I just want everyone to be as happy as I am now."

Jack gave her an indulgent look. "We're giving it our best shot."

"Good. Now, have you decided to hire Chloe as your decorator?"

Jack didn't miss a beat. "That's the plan."

Obviously startled, Chloe glanced at Jack.

"Great!" Viva said. "She's dying to get her hands on Fairhaven."

Even though Viva had beaten him to the punch, he really didn't mind. She'd given him the perfect opening. "I'm counting on Chloe's advice. As a matter of fact, I was hoping we could get started this week."

"Wednesday morning works for me," she said, not missing a beat.

That very evening appealed to him more, but he

didn't push. "It's an ideal day for me, as well. How about late morning?"

"Of course. I'll put you on my calendar for eleven. If you have a conflict, just let me know," Chloe said.

"I'll be there," Jack assured her.

TWO

At her desk in the spacious storefront that housed McNeil Interiors, Chloe sank back in her chair. She removed her glasses and placed them atop the open file in front of her. Closing her eyes, she gently rolled her head from side to side to ease the tension in her neck and shoulders.

Although it was only early afternoon, she'd been at her office since dawn, a consequence of a restless night and her preoccupation with one Jack Howell. She couldn't get her mind off the man, despite her determination to cast him aside in favor of the interiors she was trying to design for a nearby bed-and-breakfast inn. She needed to be prepared for the meeting scheduled the following afternoon with the owners of the new inn, but at the rate she was going, she feared she wouldn't be.

She exhaled, the sound rich with aggravation. Surging to her feet, Chloe made her way to one of the file cabinets that stood against a nearby wall. After jerking open a drawer, she hesitated. What was she looking for? For a long moment she wasn't even sure because her thoughts had snagged on Jack Howell yet again.

Blast the man! she thought, resenting his ability to distract her from her work.

He already posed a very real threat to her hard-won emotional balance. Chloe knew that little fact as well as she knew her own shoe size.

Finally remembering what she needed, she jerked a page of room dimensions out of the Shelby Inn file, shoved the drawer closed, and marched back to her desk. Chloe settled into her chair again, reclaimed her glasses, and studied the notes she'd made on the inn's formal living room.

She heard the sound of the shop's front door chime a short while later. Chloe glanced up, a welcoming smile on her face. Her smile dimmed, and she almost stopped breathing a heartbeat later.

Jack Howell. He stood in the doorway of her office, larger than life and just as appealing as he'd been the previous afternoon. No, she realized, even more appealing.

In khaki trousers, a navy cable-knit sweater, and all-weather boots, his attire suited the plummeting temperatures. His short-cropped dark hair was slightly ruffled thanks to a gusting breeze, and his skin had that ruddy healthy look of a man who spent time out of doors.

In short, Jack Howell looked good enough to—

Chloe bit back a groan of utter frustration as she smothered the thought, infuriated with herself for allowing him to create havoc in her brain.

Unfortunately, she couldn't ignore the desire she felt for him. The intense, I-crave-your-touch kind of desire that short-circuits a person's common sense. She'd heard about it, read about it, and fantasized about it, but she'd never experienced it before. Until now.

This man made her want things that she didn't want to want, things that could place her in a vulnerable emotional position.

Chloe stared at him, registering, not for the first time, that Jack Howell had crashed into her safe little world like a proverbial battering ram. The end result: rattled emotions and shattered composure and sensual thoughts that were erotic enough to make her blush.

Pull yourself together, she told herself as she reclaimed her poise with both hands. "Hello."

He smiled at her as he moved forward and allowed the heavy front door to close behind him. "Hello yourself."

Chloe pushed up from her chair. She didn't intend to give him the slightest advantage. She felt pretty idiotic, since her heart was tripping like a marathoner's at the finish of a long race. He was a potential client, she reminded herself, so she needed to treat him like one. "You're a surprise. I thought our appointment was for Wednesday morning."

He shrugged, the casual gesture emphasizing the

width of his broad shoulders and his leanly muscled physique. "I had a meeting in town, so I thought I'd stop by."

"Oh?" she said, struggling to contain her pleasure.

"Do you mind?" he asked, his smile fading to a look of puzzlement as he gazed at her. "I was hoping we could talk."

She remained standing. "Would you like some coffee?"

"Why don't I buy you a cup at Murphy's?" he suggested, nodding in the direction of the coffee shop across the street.

She shook her head. "Not possible, I'm afraid. My secretary called in sick this morning, and I have a client who plans to stop by this afternoon."

"No problem." He paused beside one of the chairs positioned in front of her desk. "May I?"

"Of course." Chloe sat down as well, although she stayed perched on the edge of her chair instead of settling comfortably into it.

He looked around. "I like your place."

She followed his gaze, even though she knew the exact placement of row upon row of bolts of fabric, wallpaper samples, paint color displays, carpet and tile samples, and a variety of other decorator items used in the design business. "I think of it as a study in controlled chaos."

"You have an excellent reputation as a decorator."

"How do you know?"

"I asked around."

"Makes sense, especially since you're thinking of hiring me," she conceded.

"I thought I had," Jack said softly.

I'm having very serious second thoughts. "We have to make certain that we're compatible," Chloe pointed out. "That takes a little bit of time."

"I definitely need your guidance."

She appreciated his regard for her skills as a decorator. She grudgingly gave him high marks for understanding the necessity of the harmonious use of textures and colors when decorating a mansion like the one he'd just restored. "I think I can help, and I'm particularly interested in this project," she admitted. "It'll be a wonderful challenge."

"Good." He studied her for a long moment. "I'm interested, too, by the way."

She hesitated then. The expression on his face confirmed her suspicion that he was talking about something other than decorating. She felt her heart stutter to a brief stop. When it resumed normal beating, she got to her feet and smoothed down the front of her tunic-style sweater. He stood, as well, but he didn't say anything more.

"Why don't we get some coffee and then talk about what you have in mind? If I can get a sense of your mental image of your home, then we can get started." She didn't admit that she'd already started experimenting with the color boards she used at the beginning of any new project.

"Sounds like a good plan."

As they made their way to the coffee bar at the rear of the store, she pressed her palms together and told herself to stay focused on decorating. Unfortunately, her brain and her senses had other ideas. They were too busy exclaiming with delight over the scent of his aftershave and wondering how she would feel if he placed his hands on her bare skin.

"Your other client," he began.

She gave him a blank look. It took her a minute to remember Meredith Hanover. "What about her?"

"What time is she due?"

"In a while. She has a busy schedule, so she's tough to pin down." She kept her reply vague, because she wasn't about to admit that Meredith Hanover was the least punctual of her clients. If she showed up at all that afternoon, Chloe would count herself lucky.

"Then we'll have to make every minute count, won't we?"

She gave him a bemused look. "I guess we will."

They paused in front of the antique sideboard that held the coffeemaker, containers of cream and sugar, several mugs, and a huge crystal jar filled with squares of walnut-studded fudge that she'd made the previous evening.

"I enjoyed yesterday," Jack said.

She concentrated on filling two mugs with coffee. "It was a lovely party. Typically Viva. She's the most accomplished hostess I've ever known."

"Black's fine." Jack helped himself to one of the

mugs and stepped back. "And I wasn't talking about my cousin or her hostessing skills."

Chloe gripped her own mug with both hands as she met his very direct gaze. "I know," she admitted.

"I don't mean to make you uncomfortable, but I do, don't I?"

She saw his concern in the depths of his hazel eyes and in the worry lines that creased his forehead. In the moments that followed, Chloe felt much of her resistance to him collapse like toppling dominoes. Denying the truth seemed silly, so she sighed faintly and nodded.

"Do you want me to leave?"

"I didn't mean it that way," she protested.

"You don't want me to leave," he clarified.

She hesitated, feeling even more foolish. "I'm not sure."

"Can I wait until you decide?" He smiled as he spoke, but his smile was tinged with a hint of desire that raised caution flags in her mind.

Chloe trembled all over. She scanned his rugged features. She liked him. She also wanted him. So much so that she ached.

She sensed, thanks to the warmth in his gaze, that he wanted her. Wanted her more than he probably should, she realized. She felt glad and wary all at once, and she suspected that she should do them both a huge favor and send him on his way. It would save them both time and the hassle of starting something that she knew better than to start. She hated the idea of not seeing him again, though. Genuinely hated it.

How, she wondered, could she want a man as much as she wanted Jack Howell when she hardly even knew him? She'd never really believed in that nebulous thing called chemistry. Until now.

"I'm going to take your silence as a maybe."

She burst out laughing. "I'm behaving like an adolescent. Indecision isn't my usual style."

"Makes us even."

"Why?"

"I felt like an awkward teenager yesterday."

"You couldn't have."

She recalled his composure, even as he'd told her things about himself that had surprised her. Jack Howell wanted a real home. His words had haunted her. She'd grasped the sincerity in his admission and she'd understood the desire he'd articulated. Understood it better than she wanted to admit to anyone, even herself.

"I definitely did."

"But why?"

"Because I'm lousy at this man-woman thing. It's probably one of the reasons I've been alone for most of my adult life."

Startled by his honesty, she glanced away. He reached out with his free hand and placed his fingertips against the side of her face. She stiffened, exhaled raggedly, then allowed him to nudge her face back into view. As she looked up at him she wondered if her fear was apparent. She silently cursed her deceased husband. Martin had taught her painful lessons about safeguarding her emotions. For the first time since his death, she couldn't help wondering if she'd gone overboard and become too paranoid.

He chuckled. "I put that somewhat indelicately, didn't I?"

"We're not having a man-woman thing," she insisted, her tone firm.

He fell silent. Chloe sensed that he was trying to read her thoughts.

"We aren't," she said once again for emphasis, although she suddenly wondered if she was protesting something as inevitable as the passage of time.

Jack frowned, then nodded. "Not yet, anyway."

If she lost him as a client, then so be it. "Perhaps not ever," she cautioned. A voice in her head told her that she was crazy, especially given their obvious attraction to each other. Chloe ignored the voice, and then said a quick prayer that she wasn't being totally stupid.

"If that's how things unfold."

"I'm not comfortable with some of the feelings I've had since yesterday," she said, no longer willing to pretend that they hadn't made some kind of connection. "But I meant it when I said I wouldn't be managed or manipulated."

"I'm not sure how to respond, except to tell you that the last thing on my mind where you're concerned is manipulation."

She smiled ever so faintly. She'd heard those words before, but the man who'd uttered them had been a liar. A part of her really wanted to believe that Jack Howell was different, especially since her instincts kept insisting that he was. "That was the right thing to say, as long as you're sure you won't change your mind."

"I don't say things I don't mean."

Some of her resolve deserted her. She sensed then that Jack Howell was precisely what he seemed. One of those rare individuals who spoke the truth or didn't speak at all. Still, she hesitated.

"I promise," he said quietly. "I don't use people, Chloe. And I have no plans to use you."

She exhaled shakily. "I intend to hold you to your promise."

"I expect you to."

"Now what?" she asked.

"My new home?"

"You still want me as your interior decorator?"

"Of course," he answered. "Shall we start with a contract?"

"I normally save the contract signing until we're certain that we agree on the decorating concept we'll be using and it's time to start spending your money."

"Fair enough."

"Why don't we discuss what you want?"

"Could take hours," he mused, a twinkle in his hazel eyes as he looked at her.

Let's try for years, she thought. *Oh, dear.* "It usually does," she said, hoping she sounded like a composed professional.

"How about a late lunch while we talk?" Jack suggested. "We can have something brought in, since your secretary's out today."

"I've already eaten, but I have some crackers and cheese in the kitchen if you're hungry."

"No thanks. How about lunch tomorrow?" he asked.

A business lunch, she told herself as she marveled over his persistence. Keep it simple, she silently counseled. As she studied him Chloe knew there was nothing even remotely simple about this man or their situation. She was scared to death, but she intended to move forward. *I've lost my mind*, she decided, but she suddenly suspected that being guilty of a touch of madness wasn't a totally bad thing.

"I think I'd like that."

"So would I," he said.

Set off balance by his megawatt smile, she couldn't think of anything to say. She was too busy feeling emotions she hadn't felt in years and fantasizing about what he might be like as a lover. She wanted him, she realized, even more than she'd wanted him the day before or even fifteen minutes before. Lord, help her!

"I like you, Chloe McNeil. I like you a lot."

She stared at him, then said honestly, "And I like you."

"Sounds bad when you say it that way," he teased.

She frowned. "I'm not sure what it is."

"Don't feel alone. I don't know either, but I'd like to find out."

Her hand shook. She placed her mug of sloshing coffee on a nearby table and stepped back. "I'm not in a hurry."

"I understand."

His expression assured her that he really did understand. "I won't let anyone do that to me ever again, Jack."

He nodded. "Duly noted." He paused, then shook his head.

She glimpsed regret in his angular features, although she didn't understand the cause. "What are you thinking?"

"The man who hurt you was a fool."

Chloe paled. She started to take a step backward.

Jack gently snagged her wrist, halting her retreat in mid-step. "Please don't be afraid of me."

"I'm not."

He looked doubtful. "I want to believe you."

Chloe squared her shoulders, but she made no attempt to free herself from his grasp. "I was married to a very difficult and unpredictable man. I'm more careful now. I try to think of the consequences when I meet an . . . attractive man." She shrugged. "End of story."

"Or the beginning of a story," Jack remarked thoughtfully.

"Maybe, but this isn't the time or the place to dredge up my past."

"You're right, but there's something you need to know."

"And what's that?"

"I'm not a fool, Chloe McNeil, and I don't ever intend to be one where you're concerned."

She managed a faint smile. "I hope not."

"I want to move into Fairhaven by Christmas. Is that possible?"

She laughed at his abrupt shift in subject. "I'm starting to think that anything's possible."

He chuckled. "Me too."

"Come with me, then," she urged as she led the way to one of three large worktables positioned against the wall on the far side of the huge room. "I've been playing with some ideas that you might like to see."

She paused in front of the worktable, her gaze skimming over the collection of sketches she'd already roughed out, an array of fabric and carpet swatches, and the master paint color boards she'd assembled earlier that day for his home.

His surprise apparent, Jack studied the materials she'd laid out. "For Fairhaven?"

"For Fairhaven," she confirmed, delighted by the pleasure she saw in his features.

He glanced at her. "How did you know?"

"I call it educated speculation." She didn't confess that she'd carefully studied him during their conversation at Viva and Spence's home. The end result was that she'd used his personal appearance and wardrobe, along with her knowledge of the mansion's architectural style and the landscaping being planned for the grounds of the estate, to guide her in the creation of color boards for the interior of the mansion.

"This is exactly what I had in mind."

"It's just a beginning," she warned. Her gaze fell to the array of fabric and carpet samples that she'd stapled to a large square of poster board. Teal and navy dominated, with splashes of garnet and pale rose. "Aside from the lunch hour, my day is pretty tightly scheduled tomorrow, so you'll want to take these samples with you to the house before our Wednesday-morning meeting. Your senses will help you verify whether or not you'll be comfortable with this basic color scheme when you hold it up against the woodwork in the house. Make certain that you gauge early-morning and late-afternoon light, because the impact of natural light on the fabrics in your home is very important over the long haul. If your reaction is still favorable, then we'll figure out which fabric textures appeal most to you and proceed from there."

"Very logical," Jack noted as he glanced at her.

She laughed. "You needn't look so surprised."

"You are full of surprises," he informed her. "Then what?"

"I need to get a sense of your taste in furniture, so we'll visit some showrooms in the area."

"Wednesday?"

"If you'd like. My schedule's clear in the afternoon."

He nodded. "I'd like. As I said, I want to be in the house by Christmas."

"We'll try," she promised, although she knew from experience that the odds were against them.

"About lunch."

"Tomorrow?"

"Still doable?" he asked.

She hadn't been kidding about her schedule, but she intended to take time. It was a simple matter of indulging herself, despite how dangerous it might be.

"Eminently doable. Where shall we meet?"

He hesitated. "You name the place."

"How about Murphy's?"

"The coffee shop?"

"Michael's chowder is the best around."

"Another transplant from New England?"

"Michael's wife is from Maine. Her father was in the clam business."

"Murphy's it is," Jack agreed. "I haven't had a good bowl of chowder in a long time."

Meredith Hanover, a longtime friend and client, selected that moment to burst through the front door. An ex-model with a flamboyant style all her own, she exclaimed, "I've misplaced my watch again, Chloe, and I don't know if I'm early or late."

"You're right on time, Merry, so don't give it another thought."

"See you tomorrow," Jack said, his hands full of samples and his smile wide as he made his way to the front door.

"So that's Tommy's son," Merry said as Jack strolled out the front door of the shop. "Very, very nice. Kind of like Harrison Ford, but a tad younger and several inches taller."

"I hadn't noticed," Chloe insisted as she settled into her chair and gave Merry a bland look.

"And pigs fly!" Grinning, Merry shrugged out of her coat and plopped down in a chair on the opposite side of the desk.

"He's just a client, so don't get any other ideas."

Merry laughed, her gaze direct and openly speculative. "I don't need to, since I think you already have. I'm relieved. Your personal life's been in the deep freeze since Marty died."

Chloe glared at her friend and client, then burst out laughing. "So shoot me."

"It's about time, girlfriend. You've played the wounded bird long enough. It's time for you to start enjoying your life again, and having a man around is one perk every woman needs." She winked. "Needs being the operative word."

Chloe flushed. "I'm thinking about it, so don't rush me."

Merry groaned. "You move like cold molasses going uphill, Chloe McNeil."

In response to her remark, Chloe pulled a file from the stack on her desk and flipped it open. "We have work to do. I think I've found that rosewood armoire you've been wanting for the master suite." She slid a photograph of the piece of furniture across her desk for Merry's inspection.

Her delight evident in the trademark baby blues that had sold everything from upscale cosmetics to sports cars, Merry squealed, "Bingo!"

Chloe mentally crossed her fingers that there would be no further discussion of personal matters. Merry Hanover was one of her favorite people, but only when she refrained from offering advice about Chloe's nonexistent love life.

For the time being, Chloe had enough thoughts about Jack Howell. She didn't need any more. Otherwise, she'd never get any work done or any sleep at night.

THREE

Chloe and Jack met as planned the following day for lunch at Murphy's. Once they finished a tasty meal of clam chowder, fresh-from-the-oven, hard-crust French bread, and glasses of Chenin Blanc at the tiny eatery, they didn't linger at their table out of consideration for the line of patrons waiting to take their place.

While Jack paid their lunch tab, Chloe put on her coat, collected her purse, and dug around in her pockets for her leather gloves. He slipped a few bills under the pepper mill for the waitress, who'd already begun to clear away their dishes, before he escorted Chloe through the crowded restaurant to the front door.

Jack registered the curious glances cast their way. He smiled pleasantly, making eye contact with several people. He knew the members of the community still perceived him as an unknown quantity, so he didn't fault them for their obvious interest. It reminded him once again that Tommy Conrad had been an icon in Kentucky, respected by everyone thanks to his integrity and generosity.

Pulling open the restaurant's front door, he held it for Chloe, then followed her outside. "Do you have time for a walk before you head back to the office?"

She glanced at her watch as they paused on the sidewalk. "Sounds too good to pass up, so I'll make time. I haven't been to the gym this week, and the exercise will do me a world of good."

Jack peered up at the turbulent-looking sky. Cold gusts of air sent the few remaining leaves on a nearby tree fluttering to the ground. He zipped up the front of his leather jacket.

"Looks like we might get another snowfall tonight." He glanced at Chloe.

"You may be right." After tugging on her gloves, she turned up the collar of her coat. "My grandmother always said you could smell snow several hours before it was destined to fall." She tested the theory by sniffing the air. "Definitely smells like snow to me."

Jack grinned at her as they began their stroll up Main Street. "Interesting woman, your grandmother. The National Weather Service could have used her as a consultant. What else was she able to forecast?"

She laughed. "Rain when her arthritis acted up, fog if she had a headache, and an impending heat spell if the bottoms of her feet itched. Funny thing was, she was always right, so no one in the family— or in the neighborhood, for that matter—ever dared to contradict her. She was a generous-natured woman. I still miss her, even though she's been gone for almost fifteen years now, but I treasure the wonderful memories I have of her."

"How many are in your family?"

Chloe warmed to the subject. "Three brothers and two sisters, all older, and my parents. There are so many aunts, uncles, and cousins that I've lost track of that particular statistic."

"I think I envy you." They paused at a lighted intersection. "I can't even imagine that kind of an extended family."

"I've grown to appreciate them all, but the downside when I was a little girl was that there was always a line for the bathroom."

He chuckled. "Reality check, but not an altogether unpleasant one when you consider the alternative."

"Exactly," she agreed with a smile.

"You seem very relaxed today." Jack claimed her gloved hand, and they started across the street when the light turned green.

"I am relaxed."

Jack took it as a positive sign that Chloe didn't attempt to free her hand once they reached the other side of the street. "That must mean I haven't made you uncomfortable yet today," he said casually.

She flushed. "You never really did, Jack. I'd

worked some very long hours during the last couple of weeks, and I'd been wrestling with some old issues, that's all."

"Have you been able to resolve some of them?"

As he waited for her to answer he admitted to himself that self-interest had prompted his question. He cared about her, cared a great deal, and he didn't intend to do anything to harm her, but he also wanted Chloe McNeil. Wanted her in ways he'd never wanted any other woman. For the time being, he was happy to share time with her, become better acquainted with her, although the desire he felt for her was a constant. He suspected that he was destined to feel desire for her until he took his last breath.

On some levels he knew her very well. How could he not? They'd both experienced emotional isolation, although under vastly different circumstances. They were both at a crossroads in their lives, as well, but he couldn't help wondering if Chloe even realized it.

"I don't think some personal issues are completely resolvable, Jack." She met his gaze as she finally answered his question. "But I'm working on them."

"Kind of like a work in progress?"

"We're all works in progress when you get right down to it. Some people just have a little more work to do than others. I guess I'm one of those people."

"I know how you feel."

She paused. "I think you do, which is why I'm not as defensive with you as I was yesterday."

"You'll always be cautious, though."

"True, but it's not something I'm willing to apologize for," she cautioned firmly.

"I'm not Martin McNeil, Chloe, so you don't have to explain or justify your feelings, or even apologize. I like who you are, and I certainly have no desire to change you."

She stumbled to a stop and searched his features. He withstood her inspection, understanding in his heart that she needed to be certain that he spoke the truth and be reassured that he didn't have ulterior motives and wouldn't turn the tables on her. He'd known people like that, and from what Viva had said, Chloe had been married to a man who'd turned her life into a living hell.

Jack vividly recalled the loneliness of his own youth, the years of praying that someone would want to adopt him and then the disappointment that had followed when no one stepped forward. At some point during adolescence he'd abandoned his dream of being a part of a family. Chloe, whether or not she knew it, had reawakened those dreams. He wanted a committed relationship, perhaps even a child to love.

She shook her head, and his optimism started to fade.

"I don't know quite what to say," she began.

"Whatever feels right usually works." He kept his tone neutral.

She smiled ever so hesitantly. "I believe you."

"Experience can be a ruthless teacher," Jack said quietly. "I discovered that the secret was not to become bitter."

"Amen to that," Chloe murmured.

He lifted her hand and pressed a kiss to the tips of her gloved fingers. "Thank you."

"For what?" she whispered, clearly startled by the intimate gesture.

"For believing me, and for letting me into your life."

Jack hoped that Chloe wouldn't feel compelled to backpedal or try to deny the truth of what was happening between them. He waited with the kind of patience honed by years of methodically building cases that ended with convictions. He waited for Chloe to meet him halfway. She didn't disappoint him, and pleasure surged through him when she finally spoke.

"You're welcome, Jackson Howell."

He groaned. "I gather that Viva felt the need to tell you my first name."

Smiling broadly, Chloe shrugged. "She mentioned it."

"I shudder to think of what else she decided to mention."

"Just good things."

He arched a dark brow, unaware that he looked slightly rakish despite the wire-rimmed glasses he wore.

"Scout's honor," she insisted laughingly. "Would I lie?"

He deliberately frowned. "Trust is a two-way street, so I'll refrain from taping shut my cousin's mouth."

Chloe's laughter trailed after them as they resumed their walk, fingers intertwined and palms mated. They crossed the street and made their way through the open wrought-iron gates of the six-acre city park.

Chloe and Jack strolled along the winding pathway. Despite the brisk breezes, falling temperatures, and the angry-looking clouds stacking up in the sky, Jack savored the day and the woman at his side.

"Was it difficult for you to leave the Justice Department?" Chloe asked after a while.

He shook his head. "Not really. I was ready for a change. I'd already been considering other options when Tommy and I discovered our relationship. After teaching law classes at Georgetown for almost five years on a part-time basis, I knew that I wanted to teach full-time."

"What exactly did you do at the Justice Department?"

"I was a senior investigator. I coordinated long-term criminal investigations, mostly undercover operations."

"Sounds very James Bond."

"It wasn't nearly that glamorous. The real truth is that most law-enforcement jobs are made up of long stretches of boredom interspersed with a few moments of excitement. Although I spent at least half of my time out in the field, I was also responsible for a lot of administrative details that have to be dealt with in any bureaucratic agency. The Justice Department was no exception, even though we were the good guys in white hats who were supposed to save honest citizens from the criminals."

"It doesn't seem so glamorous when you describe it that way," Chloe conceded.

"Exactly, but I still liked the work. Building a case against a felon can be tedious." He smiled at her. "Not at all the way it's portrayed on television or in the movies. There are a lot of unknowns. Those unknowns can lead to the truth, but the price along the way can be very high."

Jack paused then, his thoughts on Spence Hammond's stepbrother, Michael. A deep-cover agent for the Justice Department during a three-year investigation of a cartel responsible for several homicides, insurance scams, and money laundering, Michael had been executed when his undercover status had been discovered. Jack and his fellow investigators had eventually brought the cartel's kingpin, Daltry Renaud, to justice, but the cost of success on that particular case had been exorbitant.

Chloe spoke softly. "You're thinking of Michael Hammond, aren't you?"

Jack exhaled, then met her gaze. "Yeah. Did you know him?"

She nodded. "Very well. I also knew Daltry Renaud, but only socially. Viva and Spence confided in me after they returned from California, so I'm aware of a lot of the details surrounding the case. I gather that you met Tommy because of the investigation, but you obviously lost a good friend when Michael died."

He nodded, his mixed emotions over the case and his regret about Michael evident in his eyes.

"You did your best, Jack."

"I know, but sometimes it doesn't feel like enough."

Chloe shifted closer. "You're not God, so don't blame yourself."

"Did you blame yourself?" he asked, referring to her late husband's accident and to their marital discord.

"Yes, until someone very wisely reminded me that we all have free will. We have no control over the choices that other people make. I didn't have control over Martin's decision to drive after spending yet another afternoon in a local bar, any more than I had control over many of the other choices he made during our marriage. You had no control over Daltry Renaud, and I doubt that you could have stopped what happened to Michael."

"I have a clear conscience, if that's what you mean, but I still feel tremendous regret."

"Then ask yourself what he would want you to do," she suggested.

He smiled, although it was a smile tinged with sadness. "I already have, and the answer is exactly what I'm doing."

"Your work reminds me of a puzzle with a thousand minuscule pieces."

He nodded. "Good analogy."

"Other than your connection to Tommy, what prompted you to move here?"

"Curiosity and a desire to learn about the heritage of my birth father. Tommy didn't just leave Fairhaven and investments to me, he left personal journals, family photo albums, and a wealth of documents that date back a few hundred years. As I browse through the paperwork I'm discovering things I never even imagined existed. The Conrad family has a rich history."

"From what you've said, you've lived the life of a vagabond. Was that a factor?"

He peered at her, not at all put off by her curiosity. His reaction surprised him a little, especially given his lifelong propensity for guarding his privacy. Chloe was different, though. He felt gratified by her interest, because he wanted her to know and understand him. He hoped her curiosity would lead to other things, although he wasn't prepared to voice that hope.

"It was the only other factor, to be quite honest. I've always led a relatively rootless existence, but I hoped that would change when I moved here."

"Has it?" she asked as they strolled along the pathway.

"I feel as if I've gained a real sense of connection to my family as I've restored Fairhaven. Viva and

Spence have helped me with the transition. I owe
them a great deal."

Chloe smiled. "Something tells me they won't be
sending you a bill. Viva's too excited to have a cousin
all her own. She subscribes to the theory of the
more, the merrier."

"She qualifies as one of the most enthusiastic
people on the planet," Jack agreed with a laugh.

"Where will you teach?"

"At a law school on the outskirts of Louisville."

"Parker-Adams?" she clarified.

"That's the one."

"It has an excellent reputation."

He nodded. "A colleague from Washington introduced me to the dean of the law school a few
years ago. I let him know when I took an early re-
tirement from Justice, and he offered me a vacant
faculty position before I left D.C. Classes get under
way in mid-January."

"Is that why you want to be settled in at
Fairhaven by Christmas?"

He shrugged, a little embarrassed because of his
real reason for pushing for a quick completion on
the decorating end of the restoration. "I guess."

Pausing on the deserted pathway, Chloe studied
him with a frown. "You guess?"

"I've never actually celebrated Christmas in my
own home," Jack admitted, wondering even as he
said the words if Chloe would think him strange. "I
thought it was about time."

"It's a very special time of the year. It should definitely be enjoyed, and it should be shared."

He relaxed when he heard both the lack of censure and the gentle reassurance in her voice. "What do you usually do? Head up to Boston to be with family?"

"I have several times, but not in recent years. I like decorating a tree in my own home, going to church, listening to the carolers when they perform in the town square, and baking all the wonderful foods that are a part of the season." She grinned. "My friends accuse me of turning into a Martha Stewart clone. Last year was probably the best holiday season since my childhood," she confided as they continued walking. "I invited a local family to share Christmas with me. I have a guest house, so they stayed the night after midnight mass and spent Christmas morning with me. The father had lost his job and things were fairly difficult for the family, so I decided to play Mrs. Santa Claus."

"That was very generous of you."

Chloe shook her head. "Not really. I got back far more from the experience than I gave. I loved every moment of it." She glowed as she spoke. "The kids were wonderful. Three girls and a boy, all under the age of ten."

He recalled something that Viva had said about Chloe when they'd talked earlier that day. "You don't have children, do you?"

Her joy faded in the blink of an eye. Chloe exhaled, her breath crystallizing in the air in front of her before she answered. "No, I don't."

Her regret was too obvious to ignore. "You want them, though, don't you?"

"I've always wanted them," she admitted quietly.

"Your husband didn't?"

"Martin wasn't good at sharing."

Jack filled in the blanks, concluding that Martin McNeil had been an insecure weakling. "How long were you married?"

"A little more than eight years."

"That's a long time to be unhappy."

"We were very happy at first. We met in Boston while he was finishing his architectural studies. We moved down here when Martin's mother was diagnosed with cancer. That was about three years after our wedding. Things started to deteriorate about a year after we arrived in Kentucky. My decorating business took off like a rocket, while Martin struggled professionally. He'd had a drinking problem before I met him, although I didn't realize it. When life didn't go his way and the success he expected didn't materialize, Martin drank. He used alcohol as an anesthetic."

"Was he abusive?" Jack asked, worried that she'd been the victim of violence.

"Yes, but not in a physical sense until the last few months of his life." Chloe paused.

"Am I making you uncomfortable?"

"No, since what I'm telling you is common knowledge."

"Why did you stay with him, Chloe?"

"I didn't take my vows lightly," she said candidly. "But when he fractured my arm, I knew the marriage was over and that divorce was inevitable and necessary. The instant I realized that I wouldn't ever trust him again was when I stopped loving him. I had my first appointment with my attorney on the same day that he died. I found a message on my phone machine when I got home from the lawyer's office. Once I arrived at the hospital, I learned that Martin had died in a car wreck. Fortunately, the people he broadsided at an intersection walked away from the accident."

"That must have been a tough time for you."

"It was, but once I got beyond the shock of his death, I saw the irony of the situation. There I was filing for divorce while he was endangering lives and destroying his own. I finally came to the conclusion that God understood how tortured Martin was, and He took him so that he couldn't harm anyone else. Once I figured all that out, I was able to get on with my life."

Jack brought his hands up and framed Chloe's face. She looked somewhat bemused, but not ready to flee. He reminded himself that she had every reason to be wary. "I think you're a remarkable woman, Chloe McNeil."

She smiled, then laughed, but the sound was vaguely self-conscious. "I don't know about that."

Jack stepped closer. "Trust me then, because I do

know. The evidence is standing right in front of me."

"All right, I'll trust you."

Her eyes were so huge with surprise that Jack sensed he was destined to drown in the brilliant green pools. "He didn't deserve you."

"How can you be so sure? I might have been an absolute shrew," she teased, laughter in her voice.

Jack chuckled. "Very doubtful."

"You have a lot of faith in me, even though we hardly know each other."

He sobered. "I think we've known each other for a long time, Chloe. Haven't you ever heard the tale about kindred spirits and how they're destined to find each other?"

She shook her head. "I can't say that I have, but it's an interesting theory."

"I definitely subscribe to it now, after meeting you."

She scanned his features. Jack sensed that she was searching, as she had done before, for sincerity. He didn't rush her. He simply waited.

Still framing her face with his broad-palmed hands, he tunneled his fingers into the dense red-gold cloud of hair that capped her head and kneaded her scalp with the pads of his fingers. The silence between them lengthened. Jack felt an odd sensation pass through him, as if time stood still.

He watched Chloe's eyes fall closed. As she exhaled, the sound like a sultry purr, Jack stared at her lips, memorizing yet again the bow-shaped perfection of them. She tempted him with her vulnerability and her willingness to allow him to touch her. She tantalized him with what he perceived as her innate sensuality.

He felt a powerful current of desire, so hot that it threatened to scorch, saturate his bloodstream. He wanted her desperately at that moment, wanted her with a hunger so great that it shocked him. Then it sobered him. Chloe, he realized, was learning to trust again and, as a result, was counting on his control.

She opened her eyes and focused on him. He saw more than he expected to see. He saw desire, even though it was clouded by caution and a hint of uncertainty. He saw surprise and recognition and disbelief, as well.

"Sometimes," Jack said quietly, "all we can do is trust the things we don't understand."

"I'm not sure that I can," Chloe said.

Her voice was so low and alluring that he ached, heart and soul, with longing to possess this woman. "I won't rush you." He meant his promise.

"I won't be rushed," she confirmed before her gaze fell to his lips. She exhaled unsteadily.

His heart raced. He tried not to overreact to the invitation in the sound. "Will you try to trust whatever happens between us?"

"Why?" she asked softly.

"Because I think it might be very important."

"Jack . . ." she began, worry evident in her tone.

"Please don't, Chloe."

With that plea voiced, he lowered his head and blocked out the pale winter sun. He claimed her lips as she whispered his name. And in that simple act, he claimed Chloe McNeil. Gently. Thoroughly. Inexorably.

She sighed.

The delicate sound reminded Jack of butterfly wings. He took his time with her, drawing out each passing second.

She responded to him slowly.

He gave her all the time she needed to accustom herself to the intimacy of the moment. Exploring her with infinite care, he traced the width of her lips with the tip of his tongue, then delicately teethed her full lower lip. As he kissed her he lowered his hands to her waist and gently drew her into his embrace. The scent of her perfume intoxicated him as much as his realization that she was trembling.

His body throbbed with desire so intense that it threatened to send him to his knees. Jack lifted his head a few minutes later and peered down at her. Chloe opened her eyes. He thought she looked dazed, almost disoriented. To his relief, he saw nothing even remotely resembling fear. If anything, the expression on her face simply validated his hope that she wanted him as much as he wanted her.

Hope became reality when Chloe reached up, placed her hands on his shoulders, and pressed against him. She whispered one word. "More."

Jack answered her demand in the next heartbeat.

Lowering his head, he fused their lips, deepening their kiss and silently damning the cold weather and the necessity of heavy winter clothing. He wanted to feel her lush shape, and he longed to trace the curves and hollows of her body with his fingertips.

The image of their naked bodies intimately joy filled his mind. Shuddering, Jack fought for the kind of control that was integral to his nature, but in this instance his struggle was greater than ever before.

He slid his tongue beyond the boundary of her trembling lips and the even lines of her teeth with one goal in mind. He wanted a real taste of the woman trembling in his arms. He discovered that her passion was flavored with equal parts hesitation and curiosity, of hidden depths and barely banked desires, and of hunger and the promise that she possessed a deeply sensual nature.

Chloe tasted exactly as he'd dreamed she would taste. She tasted like perfection.

FOUR

Chloe didn't hear the footsteps of the people who stumbled upon them a few minutes later. What penetrated her consciousness was the startled quality of their laughter.

She flinched and started to jerk free of Jack's embrace, but his firm hold on her kept her still. She realized then that he was trying to shield her from the prying eyes of strangers.

She pressed her face against his neck, her respiration ragged and her eyes closed. She stifled a groan as she registered the subtle fragrance of his cologne and the warmth of his skin. It took her several moments to collect her wits.

Her heart continued to race at a breakneck pace, hammering at her ribs as though to pound home the point that she'd made a spectacle of herself in a public place. Her limbs felt like putty, but she refused to give in to the weakness she felt.

Chloe didn't protest, however, when Jack circled her shoulders with his arm and guided her along the winding path. Neither one spoke until they reached the Main Street storefront that housed her business.

Still embarrassed, Chloe turned and looked up to meet his gaze. She saw only concern in his eyes, which helped to ease the awkwardness she still felt. Unfortunately, his concern failed to slow her racing heartbeat. Jack Howell was on the verge of turning her world upside down, and she wasn't altogether sure that she should let him.

"I don't know what to say," she finally admitted.

He smiled as he removed his wire-rimmed glasses and massaged the bridge of his nose. "I do. I wish we hadn't been interrupted."

Flushing, Chloe recalled her uninhibited response to him. As he'd held her and kissed her she'd felt as though she'd been set aflame. She'd adored his tenderness and his hunger for her. She realized then that no other man had ever made her feel both desired and safe all at the same time.

"I suspect it was best that we were," Chloe remarked with a calm she didn't actually feel.

"Maybe," he conceded, replacing his glasses. "For now, anyway."

"Perhaps forever," she cautioned. "I'm not sure how I feel about what happened between us, so I won't make any promises or give you false hope."

"I'm not asking for promises, Chloe."

"Then what do you want?" She knew the question was blunt, but she needed to understand his motives.

Reaching out, he stroked her cheek with his fingertips. Chloe's eyes shuttered closed. Without realizing it, she tilted her head as he curved his palm against the side of her face.

He spoke quietly, as if to avoid drawing the attention of the people striding past them on the sidewalk. "I want a couple of things, Chloe. I want you to give us a chance. And I want you, but I think you've already figured that out. What surprised me was that you wanted me. At least, you seemed to."

"I figured it out," she said, confirming the truth of his words. The chemistry between them was a given, even if it had thrown her completely off balance. How could she not want him? she wondered. She'd never felt more alive or more shaken by a man's touch, but the idea of trusting anyone with her emotions gave her pause. She told herself that her wariness was justified. "And I did want you."

"I promised you that I wouldn't rush you. I meant what I said. I didn't plan what just occurred. It just kind of happened. To be honest, holding you and kissing you was a lot like breathing. Pure instinct."

Startled by his admission, she studied him. She knew in her heart that Jack Howell wasn't being glib. He was being himself. As real as Viva had insisted he was. And as sincere. And as candid. In truth, he seemed to possess many of the qualities she'd told herself over the years that she wanted in the man she welcomed into her life, her heart, and her bed. She exhaled, the sound betraying her uncertainty.

He removed his hand from her cheek. "You're a surprise, Chloe McNeil."

She smiled wanly. "So are you."

"Are we still on for tomorrow?"

It took her a minute to remember the appointment they'd made. It took her another full minute to make a decision as to the wisdom of following through on it. Perhaps she wasn't being wise, but she wanted to see him again. "We're on for tomorrow, but let's meet at the Cashman's Furniture Showroom instead of here at my office."

He nodded. "I know the place."

She saw the relief that flashed in his eyes, and she realized that he was vulnerable too. No one wanted to be rejected, not even a man as strong and as attractive as Jack Howell. A man who could probably have any woman he wanted. "Right after lunch would be good for me."

"You've got a date."

She almost managed a frown. "Appointment. Big difference, Mr. Howell."

"Whatever works for you, Ms. McNeil." Jack leaned down without warning a moment later and gave her a swift, hard kiss.

Lifting her hand, she pressed her fingertips to her lips. Shock resonated within her body. Desire, as well.

He grinned, looking boyish despite his forty-four years. "You didn't really expect me not to, did you?"

"You're hopeless," she accused, just barely able to quell the laughter and delight bubbling inside her.

"But charming, don't you think?"

She tried to sound stern as she answered him. "The jury's still out on that issue."

Chuckling, he said, "You're more tempting than you realize. I'm having a heck of a time not touching you right now."

She shook her head, fighting the urge to fling herself into his arms and simply surrender to the emotions flooding her heart and the desire swamping her senses. She opted to ignore his last remark. "Is the jury still out on those samples I gave you yesterday?"

"They're perfect," he said, "You're very talented at reading people."

Chloe smiled. "Nothing's perfect, but I'm glad you like them."

"There's one thing that's perfect."

She cocked her head to one side, unsure of his meaning.

"The way you taste." That said, Jack left her standing in the doorway of McNeil Interiors.

Chloe stared after him in shock, aggravated with herself because she liked what he'd said. Liked it a lot. Groaning, she pushed open the front door of the storefront and walked inside.

"How was lunch?" asked her secretary, one of

the legion of happily married matchmakers in the local community.

Immediately on her guard, Chloe said, "Great chowder." She set aside her purse, removed her gloves, and tucked them into her pockets, then shed her coat before giving Miriam a studiously blank look.

Miriam Loughlin frowned at her employer. "That's not what I meant, and you know it."

"He's a client."

"He's the first client who's ever kissed you at the front door."

She flushed, then shrugged. "He's from Washington. I guess they do things differently there."

"Chloe McNeil, you're more stubborn than a Missouri mule. Besides, you kissed him back. I watched."

Chloe grinned, then heard the strains of a subdued conversation coming from the rear portion of McNeil Interiors. Grateful for a reprieve from Miriam's well-intentioned meddling, she said, "I hope Tom and Anne haven't been waiting very long."

"About three minutes. I gave them coffee. I told them you wouldn't mind if they browsed through the sketches you prepared for today's meeting."

"Good. Why don't you go ahead to lunch? We'll be tied up for at least an hour, maybe two. Just have the answering service catch the phone while you're gone."

Miriam nodded, but the expression on her face promised additional commentary about Jack Howell.

She took a very quick breath. "I like him, by the way. I met him on Sunday at Viva and Spence's home. If he's anything like his daddy, then he has excellent genes and a conscience. You could do worse, young lady. A whole lot worse."

"Now you sound like Meredith Hanover."

She gave her employer a startled look. "I couldn't possibly sound like that woman." Miriam huffed as she picked up the phone to call the service.

Chloe smiled, because the sixty-four-year-old matron and the flamboyant twenty-eight-year-old ex-model were as different as night and day. Unless, of course, the subject was Chloe McNeil. Before Miriam could say anything more, she headed in the direction of the partitioned workroom reserved for client meetings.

Much later, Chloe couldn't decide how she managed the task, but she conducted what turned into a two-hour meeting with Tom and Anne Shelby with her usual poise and attention to detail, despite the fact that images of Jack kept popping into her head. She decided that knowing Tom and Anne for several years had helped her relax.

Jack remained on the periphery of her thoughts throughout the busy afternoon that included meetings with two other clients, but he wasn't an intrusive presence. If anything, she often felt warmed and even comforted by her thoughts of him at unexpected moments.

Chloe left the office late that evening. After carefully navigating the sleet-slickened road to her home on the outskirts of town, she fixed a light supper, watched the news, and then prepared for bed.

As she turned out the light and crawled beneath the covers, she expected yet another restless night. After sleeping deeply for several hours, she started to dream. The dreams were so vividly erotic and arousing that she felt consumed by them. Once she reached the edge of consciousness and realized that she was alone, she moaned softly in frustration. And she again wondered how she could want a man as much as she wanted Jack Howell.

Chloe forced herself to open her eyes and face the dawn as it unfolded across the early-morning December sky.

She marveled over the reawakening of her sensual nature as she went through her morning rituals. For a long time, both before and in the years since Martin's death, she'd privately worried about her ability to respond to a man ever again. Her sense of herself as a sexually expressive being had been blunted, primarily because she'd stopped trusting Martin.

Thanks to Jack, she now felt impulses and desires she'd thought lost to her forever. Chloe considered the whole situation a mixed blessing. Her senses might be on alert and her body might be hungry for satisfaction in his intimate embrace, but her emotions were fragile. She admitted to herself that she already cared for Jack. She wanted to be able to trust again, though, and she feared making another error in judgment in her personal life.

Her emotions insisted that Jack was different. So did her intellect, but she still felt anxious.

As she reasoned her way through her feelings Chloe knew she was being guided somewhat by fear of the unknown. She also realized that there was risk in every potentially fulfilling experience.

Chloe arrived on time at Cashman's Furniture Showroom, a facility that contained one of the largest selections of furnishings in the state. Decorators from throughout the region traveled to the showroom on behalf of their clients because of the variety and quality of the furniture manufactured by the Cashman family.

As Chloe wandered through the showroom she treated her senses to the array of beautiful new fabrics and furnishings on display in the warehouse-sized structure while waiting for Jack to arrive. She checked her watch several times during the next hour.

Making her way to the front of the showroom, she checked the bustling reception area and then questioned the receptionist, who provided visitors with identification badges. Once she confirmed that Jack hadn't checked in yet, she called her office and spoke with Miriam, who indicated that he hadn't contacted McNeil Interiors that morning.

She told herself then that he might have had car

trouble. But why hadn't he gotten a message to her? she wondered. Searching her briefcase, she located the notepaper on which Jack had written his hotel and cellular-phone numbers. Yet another glance at her watch told her that he was now almost ninety minutes late, so she found a bank of pay phones and placed a call to him.

He answered on the first ring. "Howell!" he barked.

Startled by his tone, she gripped the receiver. "This is Chloe. Did we get our signals crossed on the time?"

"I can't make it. Sorry."

Chloe opened her mouth to speak, but the dial tone sounded before she could say a single word. She felt as though she'd been slapped. She forcefully recradled the receiver.

Grabbing her briefcase, Chloe barely contained her outrage at Jack's rudeness as she strode across the spacious reception area, dropped her identification badge on the receptionist's desk, and then walked out of the showroom.

She trembled with a combination of anger and embarrassment by the time she reached her car in the crowded parking lot. She couldn't believe she'd actually fantasized about a relationship with the man. She also chastised herself for being gullible enough to fall victim to his charm. She calmed herself with effort before she started her car, pulled out of the parking lot, and drove to the highway.

Chloe deliberately chose a route that would lead

her past the entrance to the Fairhaven estate before she returned to her office. She planned to fire Jack Howell as a client. No ifs, ands, or buts about it. She didn't want a business relationship with him, let alone a personal one.

Guiding her car along the restored driveway of Fairhaven, oblivious to the beautiful rolling hills and newly painted white fencing that lined both sides of the two-mile stretch of drive, she reached the knoll on which the mansion had been built and spotted Jack's late-model sports car parked in the circular driveway. No other vehicles were visible, so she assumed he was alone. She parked beside his car.

Chloe left her briefcase and purse in her car. Pocketing her keys, she marched up the front steps of the three-story dwelling. The open front doors gave her pause, and she hesitated in the doorway. About to ring the front doorbell, she froze when she heard an odd sound.

At first she assumed it was a yowling cat, probably a stray, but the sustained wail that followed told her it wasn't. She reacted instinctively to the cry of distress and raced into the unfurnished mansion.

Not quite believing her eyes, Chloe stopped dead in her tracks when she reached the formal living room and found Jack Howell pacing the hardwood floors. He belatedly noticed her as he rocked the screaming infant cradled in his arms.

"Give us a minute," he said, looking remarkably calm under the circumstances.

Too surprised to speak, Chloe nodded and remained standing in the arched entryway. A few minutes later she realized that most men would have shoved a crying infant into the arms of the first woman on the scene and then promptly disappeared. As she watched him she couldn't help wondering why Jack hadn't done one or both of those things.

The baby's crying eased into a series of fatigue-laced gurgles and whimpers, then stopped altogether. Jack kept pacing and rocking the infant, although he met Chloe's curious gaze and grimly smiled at her.

She asked the obvious question in a subdued tone, not really caring that it was obvious. "Is this your child?"

He stared at her. "You're kidding, right?"

"Hardly." The single word sounded like a piece of chipped ice as it passed her lips, because she didn't consider him, his earlier rudeness, or the possibility that he'd forgotten to mention that he had a woman with a child in his life even remotely humorous.

Jack spoke firmly. "I am not the father of this child."

She cast a doubtful look at him. Perhaps a former lover had shown up without warning and presented him with his child. He seemed far too comfortable in his role as soothing protector. His entire demeanor was reminiscent of a concerned father. That thought gave her a pang, because it reminded her of how unnatural that role would have been for her late husband. "You're sure?"

"I wouldn't lie about something this important, Chloe."

She heard steel in his voice. She saw sincerity in his eyes as he looked at her. She wanted to believe him.

"I haven't been involved with a woman for more than two years, so it is impossible for me to have fathered this child. Enough said?" he asked as he approached her, still gently rocking the bundle cradled in his arms.

Chloe slowly nodded, instinct assuring her that he spoke the truth. "Who does the baby belong to? One of the workmen on Don's crew?" She hadn't seen any other cars in the driveway.

"I don't know."

"What do you mean?" she asked, glancing down at the face of the sleeping infant. Chloe reached out and smoothed a fingertip across the knuckles of the baby's tiny fist. Her heart ached as she studied the child's translucent skin, button nose, and raven eyelashes.

"Exactly what I said. I don't know the identity of the baby's mother or father. The only thing I know is that his name is Matthew."

She gave him an incredulous look. "Are you trying to tell me that someone abandoned an infant and took the time to leave a note with his name on it?"

Jack nodded. "That's the long and short of the situation."

"When . . . I mean . . . who would do . . ."

She didn't try to finish the disjointed sentence. She just shook her head in disbelief.

"Now you know how I feel," Jack remarked.

"I can't imagine anyone leaving a helpless infant alone in an unoccupied house."

"They've been left in worse places," he said, his expression bleak.

She read the newspapers and watched the news, so she knew exactly what he meant. "What are we going to do?" she asked.

He smiled, but it was a pale imitation of his usual smile. "We?"

Chloe didn't hesitate. Nor did she care that she probably sounded like a woman who'd spent years longing for children of her own, since that was precisely who and what she was. "I'll help in any way that I can."

"There are two bottles of what looks like formula in the diaper bag in the kitchen, but the appliances aren't installed yet."

"What about hot water?"

Jack gave her a puzzled look. "The utilities were turned on last week. The water heater's working, but there aren't any pots or pans in the kitchen. My household goods aren't due to arrive for a few days."

She smiled. "No problem."

Jack followed her into the kitchen, where she turned on the tap and waited for it to get hot. After checking the contents, which looked and smelled exactly like the formula Viva was using for her new baby, Chloe held the bottle under the flow of water to warm it.

Still cradling the sleeping infant, Jack stood beside her at the sink.

Chloe gazed at the two of them. Jack, big and sturdy, seemingly fearless. The baby, tiny, probably no larger than six or seven pounds, and totally dependent on others. The contrast between the two, one strong and the other fragile, brought tears to her eyes. In an ideal world, she would have had a husband and children to love and nurture, but the world was often less than ideal, she'd discovered. Chloe blinked the tears away as quickly as possible, but not quickly enough.

"Problem?" Jack asked quietly.

She looked up at him, her eyes still swimming and her heart on the verge of breaking. Chloe cleared her throat and struggled for control. "How could anyone part with such a treasure?"

Jack didn't answer her, but Chloe didn't spend much time wondering why. Baby Matthew awakened and loudly announced his hunger.

FIVE

A short while later Jack handed Chloe the empty bottle. She draped a folded length of paper toweling from a roll left in the kitchen across his shoulder. After shifting the baby into an upright position that properly supported his head, he gently massaged the infant's upper back in a soothing circular motion with the palm of his hand.

"I'm impressed," Chloe remarked, looking quite bemused as she rinsed the bottle, set it aside on the kitchen counter, and watched the two. "Most men would have taken a hike by now."

"You've found me out, I guess."

"What exactly have I found out?"

Jack chuckled. "I really like kids. When Viva threatened to hire me as a nanny, I decided to teach Spence a few of the finer points of baby care, so the pressure's on him now."

"That seems appropriate, since he's the daddy."

Little Matthew selected that moment to vouch for Jack's competence by releasing a noisy, formula-scented burp.

Chloe grinned. "Viva isn't one to argue with success."

Her comment was promptly punctuated by a second, equally noisy gust of air. Both adults laughed.

Jack shifted the baby off his shoulder and held him so that his head remained elevated. "I had a case six years ago that involved a young woman who was trying to break her ties to the mob. She was pregnant with triplets. I wound up delivering the three babies and then helping her care for them until we could transfer them to a secure environment. It took about two weeks to get the situation sorted out, so I received a crash course in infant care."

Wide-eyed, Chloe said, "Please tell me that you delivered triplets with the help of a doctor."

Jack kept rocking the baby. Chloe watched as the infant's eyelids drifted closed.

He kept his voice low as he answered her. "We were in a remote location, and there was no time to get her to a hospital, so we improvised. We used a speaker-style telephone, and an obstetrician from the D.C. area guided us through the actual delivery. Kate did the real work, of course. I was just along for the ride and a few chores."

She shook her head, her amazement evident. "You were incredibly lucky that nothing went wrong."

"Believe me, I know. I was ill-prepared for what

happened, but the good news is that the boys each weighed almost six pounds and they were healthy. I'd had a few Red Cross first-aid courses over the years, but whatever I knew about emergency medical care disappeared when she calmly announced that her water had broken and that her sonogram had revealed triplets. I wanted to be anywhere but that isolated lodge in the Minnesota woods."

"I gather you were working undercover then."

Jack nodded. "We were attempting to keep Kate alive so that we could get her into court as our star witness."

She leaned against the counter's edge. "I assume you were successful."

"Yes, despite a few close calls." Jack remembered Kate with great fondness. He also recalled the ruthless men who'd tried to kill her, not once but several times. "I'm godfather to the three boys. Kate and her husband and their brood live up in the Pacific Northwest now. She married one of the other investigators on the case. They had twins a few years after their wedding."

Glancing down at the baby, Jack saw that he was sucking on his fist and sleeping peacefully. He crossed the kitchen, carefully settled him into the infant carrier positioned atop the counter, and tucked a receiving blanket around his tiny body.

Jack had discovered the baby securely strapped into the carrier, along with a diaper bag. Luckily, the bag had contained the note that provided his name and the message *Take care of him, please*, two bottles of formula, a plastic rattle, and a half-dozen disposable diapers, one of which he'd already used.

Once he'd gotten beyond his initial shock of finding a newborn on his front steps, he'd grudgingly given the mother, whoever she was, credit for at least providing the essentials. Jack chose to view them, and the meticulous condition of the infant and his clothing, as evidence about her concern for his welfare.

His common sense told him that, in most cases, only a desperate mother abandoned her child. His own personal history prompted an altogether different emotional response, however, but he'd managed to quell it in order to focus on the child's needs.

Chloe joined him, her gaze on the slumbering infant. Reaching out, she trailed her fingertips along the edge of the carrier, but she didn't touch the baby.

Jack frowned. As they stood together in silence, the only sound in the room the steady breathing of the baby, he slipped his arm around Chloe's waist. When he tugged her close, she stiffened. Jack felt the resistance slowly ease out of her. Only then did she allow herself to relax against him.

"What are you thinking, Chloe McNeil?" he wondered aloud.

Turning her head, she peered up at him. "I'm not really thinking right now."

He felt the sweep of her gaze as she scanned his face. He noticed what seemed to be a flash of confusion in her eyes as she studied him.

Jack considered his options. He respected Chloe's privacy, but his instincts told him that she needed an opening that would allow her to express her emotions. What she didn't need, he was certain, was to be rescued. She was a strong woman, and a proud one, as well, and he had no desire to undermine her.

"I don't want to make you uncomfortable, but can you tell me what you're feeling?" he asked.

She met his gaze. Her chin trembled, and she sank her teeth into her lower lip in an obvious effort to regain control over herself. "I'm feeling more than I can put into words," she admitted after a long pause. "There are times when I wish—" Her voice broke, and she cleared her throat before she continued, "There are parts of my life that I wish I could change, that's all."

Jack tugged her even closer. He understood regret, having wrestled with it often enough in his life. The fact that he cared about Chloe simply heightened his sensitivity to her. He suspected then that her conflicted feelings were rooted in her disappointing marriage.

Despite his concern for her, Jack felt heat stealing into his veins as he held her. He couldn't be near her without wanting her, he realized not for the first time. And he wanted her in ways that continued to surprise him.

She stared up at him. He had the impression that she was holding her breath in anticipation of what he might do next. Because he saw nothing that resembled fear or anxiety in her features, he leaned down.

She blinked, but she didn't pull back. After exhaling shakily, she didn't move a muscle. She simply watched him.

Jack interpreted her behavior as permission, but he still paused a few inches from her lips. At that moment he knew that if the price for another taste of her was his soul, he'd willingly relinquish it. His heart threatened to deafen him as he watched her moisten her lower lip with the tip of her tongue.

Moisture glistened invitingly. Seduced by the innocently erotic gesture, Jack observed, "Sometimes wishes come true, but you need to be patient until they become real."

"You're probably right," she whispered. Her eyes fell closed. Lifting up on tiptoe, she pressed a kiss to his lips.

He took what she offered very gently at first, but hunger swept over and through him like a flash fire just seconds later. He gave in to the desire he felt by deepening their kiss.

Jack craved every intimacy possible with her in the same way that a starving man craves food. Darting his tongue into the sultry depths of her mouth, he claimed her as primitive impulses surged like a storm-tossed tide into his bloodstream.

She answered his passion with her own. Turning within his embrace, her full breasts brushed against his chest as she lifted her arms and tangled her fingers at his nape. She angled her head and made her mouth even more accessible to his exploration. She tantalized his senses and his imagination with the lushness of her body, and she caused him to feel the kind of hunger that comes from both emotional and physical needs too long neglected.

Chloe then instigated a sensual mating ritual with her teasing, darting tongue. She tortured Jack even more as she undulated against him. He felt the invitation of her body as she arched into him. She kneaded the width of his shoulders with her fingers, then stroked her palms down his back.

Her mouth grew avid. They plundered each other's senses. His body throbbed with desire barely held in check.

Bringing his hands up, he slid them beneath the jacket she wore and covered her breasts with his palms. She moaned into his mouth. Lightninglike streaks of sensation scissored through him. The muscles of his body felt like tightly strung piano wire.

He stroked her, the silk of her blouse and sheerness of her bra aiding and abetting his discovery of her taut nipples. Inarticulate sounds escaped her as he flicked his thumbs back and forth across the hard tips.

Jack savored Chloe's unrestrained response. She was more volatile than he'd imagined possible, and he struggled not to lose control. He didn't want their first time together as lovers to be a hasty experience that she might regret.

Jack promised himself that when the circumstances were right, he would go slowly with her. He wanted the luxury of time. Time to explore Chloe. Time to discover what pleased her. Time to repeatedly entice her to journey beyond the edge of reality and into a world dominated by pure sensation.

Gripping her waist with both hands, he brought her lower body into intimate alignment with his hard loins, teasing them both with the promise of what they would eventually share. Caging her hips between his hands, he shifted against her. Back and forth, back and forth, until his flesh ached so much that it tested both his sanity and his self-control.

Desire exploded like tiny starbursts within his body. His carnal thoughts produced a series of erotic images in his mind. Slanting his mouth over hers, he ate at her lips with a hunger unlike anything he'd ever known before. He explored her so thoroughly that they were both gasping for air within a few moments.

More images flooded his mind. He longed to have Chloe naked and in his bed. He wanted to bury himself in the heat and softness of her shapely body. He wanted to sink into the scalding heat of her passion until his senses became saturated with her very essence and his body reached fulfillment.

Jack realized then that they had to stop, although he hated the idea of releasing Chloe even for a moment. He promised himself that he would, though. Soon. He needed just a little more of her.

She suddenly went very still in his arms. She

eased her lips free and bowed her head, resting her forehead against his chin.

Jack didn't try to stop her. Her labored breathing and her trembling body told him that she was shaken by what they'd just experienced.

As he held her and tried to get his own respiration under control, Jack knew in his heart that Chloe was a forever kind of woman. The kind of woman he'd fantasized about his entire adult life, but had doubted existed. At least for someone like him.

He closed his eyes, torn between his own physical frustration and his conviction that Chloe deserved a man capable of putting her needs first. He consciously resisted the desire pummeling his senses, and it started to recede, but very slowly.

Still so aroused that he hurt, Jack hugged Chloe, dropped a kiss on the end of her nose, and forced himself to loosen his hold on her. "I can't remember ever wanting a woman as much as I want you."

Chloe stared up at Jack. When she began to move backward, he caught her by the shoulders. He saw the shock and disbelief in her huge green eyes before his gaze fell to the kiss-swollen condition of her lips.

Desire for her spiked within him yet again. He swallowed the groan welling inside him.

"I've never . . ." She paused, then managed, "I don't understand what's going on. I'm not usually so . . ." Her voice trailed off.

"Maybe we aren't supposed to understand," Jack

speculated aloud as he realized just how explosive their attraction to each other was.

Chloe exhaled, the sound uneven and filled with vulnerability. "Maybe not," she conceded. "I'm not really sure of anything right now."

Turning in the circle of his arms, she reached out to the baby, who remained oblivious to the sensory storm that had taken place between Chloe and Jack. She placed a shaking hand atop his blanket and smoothed her fingertips over his tiny form.

Jack slipped his arms around her waist, grateful that privacy she trusted him enough to lean against him, grateful as well that she'd overcome her reserve where little Matthew was concerned. He knew the little boy needed them both, although he wondered if Chloe understood just how much.

They stood together in silence for several minutes, watching the baby sleep. Jack was struck anew by the child's innocence and dependence.

His heart sank a little in the minutes that followed, because he knew the baby's possible destiny if his mother didn't step forward to reclaim him. And if she did return for him, Jack knew there would be serious questions about her competence. Either way, Matthew had what could only be called an uncertain future.

Chloe's gaze swept over the raven-haired infant, lingering to admire the shape of his head, the delicate lines of his face, and his little fists and perfect fingers. "He can't be more than two or three weeks old."

Jack nodded. "The umbilical cord's still attached, so I suspect you're right."

She sighed, the sound filled with regret. "As much as I'd like to take him home and keep him forever, I guess we'd better contact the authorities."

Jack flinched. "No," he said, his voice as sharp as a blade.

The infant stirred, frowned, and then settled back into slumber.

Muttering a word that he rarely used, Jack released Chloe and strode across the kitchen. He stopped walking when he reached the breakfast nook, but his frustration persisted.

When he heard Chloe's footsteps on the hardwood floor of the empty room, he turned and faced her. His expression forbidding, he met her gaze.

"We don't have any other choice," she said, pausing several steps away from him.

The lawyer in him knew she was right, but the man loathed the reality. So did the small boy buried deep inside who had suffered the neglect of a bureaucratic agency designed to guard his welfare. He'd been fed, clothed, and housed, but that was all.

"You look very angry," she observed quietly.

"I'm not angry," Jack lied, although not deliberately. His denial was pure reflex, an enduring habit he'd learned as a boy. Deny the loneliness, and it would go away. It never had, though. He swore again.

Chloe appeared unruffled. "The expression on your face says otherwise. So does your tone of voice." She studied him for a long moment. "Would you like to tell me what's going on?"

"He could end up in foster care." *Just like me*, Jack thought, frustrated in advance by a system that he knew far too well. Overwhelmed and under-staffed, the Social Services system tried, he knew, to do what was best for abandoned and orphaned children, but it failed more often than he cared to recall.

"I don't like that possibility any more than you do, but what other choice do we have?" Chloe questioned. "If we have another option, I'd be happy to hear it."

Jack didn't have an answer for her. At least not yet. "Do you know a good pediatrician?" he asked instead.

"Of course. Tom Hansen. Viva is happy with him, and he's nearby."

"Then let's start with Dr. Hansen. While Matthew No-Last-Name gets the once-over, we can try to figure out a temporary solution for him." He paused for a moment, then said in a harsher-sounding voice than he realized, "Social Services is a last resort, Chloe. I want that understood. If you don't agree, then tell me now, and I'll deal with the baby by myself."

Chloe slowly closed the space that separated them. She stopped less than a foot from where he stood. "Jack, I'm not the enemy. I meant it when I said we were in this together. That little boy needs both of us, but he needs us to be very calm and very smart."

He shoved the fingers of his right hand through his cropped dark hair. He was exasperated with himself. "You're right, and I apologize. I was way out of line."

"Apology accepted." Smiling, she took one last step.

Although a little surprised by her behavior, he embraced her without hesitation, his arms like bands of steel as he brought them around her and hugged her. "Thank you."

She leaned back and looked up at him. "You're very welcome."

"You're amazing, Chloe McNeil."

"Not really, but I'm glad you think so." After giving him a lingering kiss, she stepped away. "You're much too tempting, even in light of the fact that you stood me up this afternoon. I've decided to forgive you for that, though, so your apology is doing double duty."

Jack shook his head, genuinely embarrassed. "I'd forgotten."

She laughed. "So had I until a few minutes ago."

SIX

Chloe used Jack's cellular phone to call the pediatric clinic. She learned that office hours were over for the day, but the doctor promised to wait for them.

They protected Matthew from the cold weather with Jack's shearling jacket. Chloe held him as Jack drove the short distance to the clinic.

As she watched the infant smile in his sleep, she sighed softly. She also gave in to the inevitable and completely fell under his spell. No one, Chloe realized, but this innocent newborn could have captured her heart with such ease.

Tom Hansen met the trio at the front door and escorted them directly into an examination room. A tall, attractive man with twinkling blue eyes and an infectious grin, the fortyish doctor wore a pullover sweater, jeans, and running shoes. His signature bright orange stethoscope was looped around his neck, and a collection of lollipops protruded from the breast pocket of his unbuttoned lab coat.

Chloe knew him casually and liked him thanks to several social functions that they'd both attended since his arrival in the area a few years earlier. She greeted him and then introduced Jack. After the two men shook hands, Tom immediately turned his attention to Matthew, who slept soundly in Chloe's arms.

"He had his last bottle about an hour ago," she said as she relinquished the infant to the doctor. "I think the formula is the same one that Viva's been using."

He nodded. "Did I misunderstand you when you called a little while ago?"

Chloe looked at Jack.

He took her cue. "You didn't misunderstand, Doctor. We don't know the identity of the parents."

"Call me Tom, please. Why don't you start at the beginning?" he suggested. He placed Matthew on the examination table, then carefully peeled away the blanket that swaddled his tiny body.

"I found him on the front steps of the main house at Fairhaven." As he spoke Jack set aside the heavy winter jacket that they'd used to protect Matthew from the plummeting temperatures.

Tom listened as he undressed the infant. Chloe liked his gentle manner, noting that he managed to disrobe the baby without disturbing his sleep.

She glanced at Jack, who stood beside the examination table. His concern for the baby was evident in his furrowed brow and in his low voice as he recounted the events of the afternoon.

She watched him slide a single finger into the baby's open hand. A still-sleeping Matthew closed his hand around it. She heard the audible sigh that escaped him a few seconds later. The sound echoed trust.

With tears stinging her eyes, Chloe reflected on the true meaning of trust even as she wrestled with her own emotions and marveled yet again at Jack's protective attitude. She studied him as he explained his discovery of the infant, and she found herself in the position of pondering Jack's ability to inspire trust.

Chloe trusted him. Every instinct she owned assured her that he was a man of integrity and honor. She had sensed those things about him since their first moments together, she realized. She still didn't completely understand why, since she was normally quite reserved in her judgments of most people, especially men. But she'd known from the start that Jack was an unusual man, even though he'd upended her orderly little world in a multitude of ways.

Her first impression of him endured as she watched and listened to him now. Sensitive, intelligent, and too sexy for words, Jack Howell wasn't as jaded or edgy as many of the people she'd known over the years who worked in law enforcement. If anything, he seemed vulnerable at unexpected moments, in spite of his obvious strengths.

He's too good to be true, cautioned her wary heart.

Everyone has flaws, so you'd better figure out what his are before you get in over your head.

Chloe frowned. Was Jack Howell the kind of man she wanted in her life now that she'd recovered from her years with Martin? she wondered. Jack, without saying a single word, already had her yearning for the courage to risk finding out.

Would she be able to make the leap necessary for a committed relationship? Did Jack even want commitment from a woman? Or was he simply in the market for an affair?

Lots of questions, Chloe mused, but no real answers. At least not at the moment. Real answers took time. But did she want to invest the time?

She was tempted. So tempted that she ached with equal parts of hope and anxiety. She also ached physically, thanks to the lingering aftershocks of the desire she'd experienced with him.

Desire for Jack. Desire to abandon the restraint that had been a hallmark of her life. Desire to rediscover the joy of physical and emotional intimacy in the arms of a man she cared about. And she cared about Jack Howell. She was honest enough to admit to herself that she already cared more about him than she'd expected to care about anyone ever again.

The flip side of her desire for him was her refusal to be dominated. Martin's legacy again. It crept up on her at the worst times. Exhaling shallowly, Chloe knew then that overcoming her fear would be the final hurdle in putting to rest, once and for all, the ghosts of her past.

"He appears to be in excellent health." Tom set aside his stethoscope as Matthew stirred and opened his eyes. "I'd like to do some lab work on him to be certain, though, and we'll need his blood type."

Chloe snapped back to the present. This was hardly the time to worry about herself. "We think Matthew is two or three weeks old," she said as she moved forward to stand beside Jack. She cupped her hand around the baby's head, savoring his warmth as she touched him.

"Good guess. Two weeks makes sense given his size and the condition of the cord." Tom met Jack's gaze. "His name is Matthew?"

Jack nodded. "There was a note in his diaper bag. It gave his first name and asked that he be taken care of. No signature, though. It was written on a piece of torn notebook paper."

"You're an investigator and an attorney, aren't you?"

"I was with the Justice Department for several years, but I'm not licensed to practice in Kentucky. I'll be teaching law after the Christmas holidays."

"It would appear that he's been abandoned. The question is why."

"I wish we knew," Chloe said.

Tom speculated, "My guess would be an unwed mother, probably high-school age. She apparently believed that she had no other choice but to give up her child."

"Have you ever examined him before?" Jack asked.

"No, I haven't, but this is a rural area, and a lot of babies are born at home. Many of them don't see a pediatrician until there's a medical crisis of some kind."

Chloe tucked the blanket around Matthew. He looked around, gurgled his approval, then blew a few bubbles for good measure. She grinned, captivated by his good-natured behavior.

"What does Bill Sturgis think?"

Jack's silence prompted her to admit, "We haven't called Sheriff Sturgis yet."

"That's the first order of business, then." He turned and lifted the receiver of a nearby wall phone. "Get Sheriff Sturgis on the line for me." Tom explained the situation in succinct terms once his call went through to the sheriff at his office, which was just down the block. "Thanks, Bill." He recradled the phone and turned to face Chloe and Jack. "He's on his way."

"I'm aware of the law, Doctor, but I'd like to explore options aside from the obvious one."

Chloe heard the tension in Jack's voice. She wished she understood its origins, because she felt certain that Jack's concern for Matthew went far deeper than she'd originally thought. She also sensed that he had a personal stake in the infant's well-being. But if he wasn't the father, then why was he so concerned?

"Then you know it's my legal obligation to contact the local authorities when a child has been abandoned, harmed in some way, or if I suspect that he's an abductee. Social Services can't be bypassed, but the actual decision is up to Bill once he's evaluated the situation."

"We know you have responsibilities, but we're concerned about the baby's welfare," Chloe affirmed as she glanced at Jack.

She reached for his hand and squeezed it, needing his strength but also wanting to reassure him that she understood and shared his feelings. She saw the muscle ticking in his clenched jaw. He said nothing more, though. She knew then what she needed to do, but she decided to bide her time until the sheriff arrived.

Her experience as a longtime resident of the area reminded her that Bill Sturgis was a reasonable man. He would make a judgment about Matthew based on compassion and the facts that were presented to him.

The sheriff strolled into the pediatric clinic just as Tom Hansen finished withdrawing blood for the lab. While Chloe comforted little Matthew, Jack stepped forward to introduce himself to the sheriff.

Sheriff Sturgis inspected Matthew and smiled. "Good-looking boy. From what the doc said on the phone, someone left him on your porch."

"It would appear that way."

The sheriff frowned. "You think something else happened?"

"I honestly don't know. If this is a straightforward case of abandonment, then the evidence adds up. If it's not and he was dumped after being ab-

ducted, then we'll know fairly soon. The FBI and
the National Center for Missing and Exploited Children
are generally the first two agencies to be noti-
fied, and the media is inclined to run with stories
about newborn abductions as soon as they occur."

"I haven't had anything come across my desk yet
today, so why don't we sit tight on the abduction
theory. In the meantime I'll photograph this little
guy while I'm here and notify the appropriate state
and federal agencies. I'll also start canvassing the
hospitals in the surrounding counties. I dread dealing with the media, but I'll give them a heads-up
too."

"What about Matthew?" Chloe asked.

"First things first, Chloe." Bill looked at the doctor. "You've done the usual tests?"

Tom nodded. "I'll drop the blood sample at the
hospital lab on my way home."

"Good." He brought his attention back to Chloe
and Jack. "We've got a problem, I'm afraid. Lisa
Hampton's out of town for a couple of weeks on
family business. She's the sum total of Social Services for our area since Charlotte Ridgewood re-
tired. It would appear that I'm going to have to have
one of my men transport our little friend here up to
Louisville for safekeeping while we try to figure out
who he belongs to."

"I'd rather you didn't," Jack said, his emphatic
tone drawing the eyes of everyone in the room.

Even the baby stopped kicking his feet and wav-
ing his arms as he stared up at Jack.

Tom Hansen frowned.

The sheriff's reaction was less apparent, so Chloe didn't waste time trying to figure it out. "Are there any other options, Bill?" she asked.

"Anything we decide to do will probably just delay the inevitable."

"I don't agree," Jack remarked.

"That's apparent, Mr. Howell." Bill studied him, his gaze speculative. "Would you care to tell me why?"

Jack smiled grimly. "I know the system."

"Is he your son?"

"He is not, but that isn't the point," he insisted.

What *was* the point? Chloe wondered.

"We both know I had to ask. And we all know that this isn't the big city, so I can be a tad more flexible about what happens to the boy, at least for the time being." He focused on Jack, his own expression unflappable. "You still haven't answered my original question."

"I grew up in that system," Jack said.

Startled, Chloe slashed a glance at him. She'd assumed that he'd been raised by his mother. More proof that assumptions weren't always accurate, she decided. "Just how flexible are you prepared to be, Bill?"

"Let's just say that I have a lot of discretion in cases like these," he answered, clearly unwilling to be pinned down to a specific course of action just yet.

"Are there any families in the local community who are certified for infant foster care?" Jack asked.

"There are only a handful, and I know for a fact that they're full up. It's the time of year when we have our share of domestic disputes. It's tough on the children involved."

Jack exhaled, the sound harsh. Chloe shifted a step closer to him, his revelation about his childhood still rocking her.

Jack pressed in a firm voice, "I don't want him in foster care. I wouldn't wish that system on a stray pup, let alone a two-week-old infant."

"Are you married, Jack?" Bill Sturgis asked evenly.

"No, I'm not."

"Might be kind of tough for a bachelor to take care of a little tyke like this one."

"I'm willing to try."

"It's pretty out of the ordinary. And it could be a lot of work," Bill observed. He glanced at Chloe, but he didn't say anything.

"I'll hire whatever help I need," Jack said.

"You're living in a hotel, aren't you?"

Chloe wasn't surprised by Bill's question. He was a man who took his job seriously, and as a result, he was aware of everything that went on in the county.

"I can arrange to move into Fairhaven ahead of schedule. Renting furniture isn't that tough to do."

"Why go to so much trouble?" Bill asked.

Chloe knew his question wasn't out of line. She wondered why, as well.

"It's the right thing to do." Jack said the words calmly.

Chloe doubted that anyone in the room missed the intensity underscoring his remark. Or his sincerity. He was an even more honorable man than she'd thought.

Chloe suddenly realized that Jack was trying to do for Matthew what no one had done for him. Her heart broke for him and what he must have endured as a child.

As determined to protect Matthew as Jack, although for different reasons, she crossed her fingers and said a little prayer before she spoke. "Jack wouldn't be taking care of the baby by himself, Bill. In fact, I have plenty of room at my house, and I think we can put a nursery together without too much trouble."

He observed, "You're a busy woman, Chloe, what with your business and all."

"I'm not too busy to take care of Matthew," she said. "I want to do this, Bill. Will you help us?"

Although he still looked as if he'd been thrown slightly off balance by Chloe's proposal, Jack slid his arm around her waist. "We can manage for however long he needs us."

"Tom?" Bill peered at the pediatrician. "Anything you want to contribute to this discussion before I make a decision?"

"Just one thing." He focused on Chloe and Jack. "Your hearts are in the right place, but it's easy to get overly attached in situations like this one. The emotional price could be very high for both of you. I've seen it happen."

"Tom, Jack and I are willing to do whatever is necessary for Matthew. Isn't that more important than how we might feel once his mother is found?" she asked.

Jack reinforced Chloe's comments by placing his hand on Matthew's chest when the baby started to fuss. His touch immediately calmed him, and he resumed his gurgling.

Bill nodded, his amusement obvious. "I kind of think these two are already in over their heads, so that's probably a moot point. Chloe's right, though. She and Jack are adults, and they're obviously smart enough and stable enough to work out the emotional kinks once this little fella's back with his folks."

"Was that a yes, Bill?" Chloe asked.

"That was a yes," the sheriff confirmed, smiling broadly. "All right then, folks. It looks as though we've got a workable situation about to commence. Your job is to take care of this young man. Meantime, I'll protect your privacy where the media's concerned, and I'll do my darnedest to find his parents. There's a fund for foundlings. The county clerk handles it, so if you need anything, just say the word."

"That won't be necessary," Jack said when Bill paused.

"I didn't think so." Bill's expression grew thoughtful. "Tommy would have stepped in and done what you're doing if he'd been faced with the same situation. He was a fine man, Jack, and a very good friend. I'm glad to know that his son is cut from the same cloth."

Jack genuinely smiled for the first time since arriving at the pediatric clinic. "Thank you, Sheriff." He dug out his wallet and extracted a business card, which he handed to the sheriff. "You can locate me at any time by using the pager number on the back of this card."

Chloe gathered the baby into her arms as Tom and Bill left the exam room. As she rocked Matthew her emotions ranged from the pleasure of holding the baby to stark terror, the latter feeling caused by the fact that she had little or no experience as a surrogate mother.

"You'll do fine, so quit worrying," Jack said as he slid his arm around her shoulders.

Looking up at him, Chloe laughed. "Am I that obvious?"

"Let's just say I recognize the look on your face. Kate told me that all I had to do was use my common sense. Luckily, she was right."

"I guess we'd better get him dressed and go shopping," Chloe remarked as she placed the baby on the examination table and reached for the undershirt and romper that Tom had removed. "We need more supplies than you can imagine."

Jack smiled. "I bow to your feminine instincts, Ms. McNeil."

"Smart man," she answered with a grin.

His humor faded as they looked at each other. "Thank you," Jack said quietly.

"For what?" Chloe asked as she held the baby still with gentle hands.

"For volunteering. You didn't have to."

"Did you really think I'd stand by and watch him be given to strangers?"

"I hoped not, but I didn't want to put you in an awkward position." Jack paused, removed his wire-rimmed glasses, and massaged the bridge of his nose. "Something you said yesterday gave me the impression that children were a real issue for you when your husband was still alive. I guess I was afraid that it would be too hard for you."

"It would have been a few years ago," she admitted, not surprised by his observation. She'd pretty well admitted that Martin had thwarted her dream—a dream she hadn't completely relinquished yet—of becoming a mother. "When you know me better, you'll realize that we share the same fatal flaw."

He gave her a curious look before comprehension dawned in his features. "You like kids?"

Chloe nodded. "Especially babies, even though I don't have any real experience at taking care of them."

"Trust me, Chloe. We'll be a good team."

"From your mouth to God's ear," she quipped.

"You're the expert, Mr. Howell, sir, so if I have a problem, you're definitely going to know about it."

Matthew let out a squeal. Once Chloe realized that it was simply a bid for attention, she relaxed and finished dressing him. It seemed perfectly natural to her that Jack helped every step of the way.

SEVEN

"Still feeling overwhelmed?" Jack asked as he walked into the kitchen at Chloe's house that evening.

She turned and smiled at him after replacing the lid on a pot of simmering marinara sauce. "Not anymore."

She didn't mind, she realized, that he'd understood her mixed emotions of earlier in the day. Even if they were partnered in the task, taking responsibility for an abandoned infant presented both emotional and situational challenges.

Chloe appreciated the fact that Jack hadn't judged her somehow deficient because she'd had doubts about her abilities. His steadiness and his absence of judgment had allowed her to make a calm decision—the right decision, she knew. He'd known instinctively what she'd always known about herself. When she made a commitment, she carried it through. She wasn't a halfway person. She never had been, and she never would be.

"We've got some major work ahead of us tonight." Chloe glanced meaningfully at the shopping bags and boxes piled high on the couch in the adjacent family room.

They'd shopped with a vengeance after leaving the pediatrician's office, filling both of their cars with a multitude of baby-related items necessary for a temporary nursery. Because Matthew had slept his way through the experience in his infant carrier, they had accomplished a great deal in a short amount of time. Several of the items they'd purchased required assembly. She suspected that they would be busy for most of the evening.

Jack's gaze lingered on the mountain of purchases. "I noticed some of the tools we'll need on the workbench in the garage."

"Why don't we relax and have dinner first?"

"I don't think I've ever had a better offer." He made his way to the stove, lifted the lid, and inhaled deeply of the fragrance of simmering sauce before replacing the lid. "Smells great. You're a very talented woman, Chloe McNeil."

She laughed. "Thank you, but I have to confess that when I was a little girl my best friend was Italian. Her parents owned a restaurant in the north end of Boston, so we spent a lot of time underfoot in the kitchen when we weren't terrorizing the nuns at St. Dominica's. Her mother put us to work as a deterrent, but it didn't take. We were absolutely thrilled even when we were busing tables. Rosalie became one of Boston's most successful caterers, and I learned some valuable lessons along the way."

"Something tells me you're being far too modest."

"Not really. Rosalie's the genius. I just love good food." After stirring the contents of a second pot, this one filled with boiling pasta, Chloe moved to the sink to fix a salad to go with their meal. "How's our little friend?"

"Sound asleep. I put him on the bed in your room until I can get his bassinet set up."

As he spoke Jack collected the plates, silverware, and napkins stacked on a nearby countertop. He walked to the oak trestle table that separated the kitchen and the family room.

Chloe noticed how masculine he made the simple task of setting the table appear, then silently chastised herself for being silly. Any man who'd been a bachelor all of his adult life had to have acquired a few domestic skills. Still, she appreciated his willingness to pitch in and help without being asked. In her experience as a daughter, sister, and wife, his behavior was definitely unusual.

Jack rejoined her as she stood at the sink. When he placed his hands on her shoulders and gently massaged them, she put aside the tomato she'd just rinsed and let her head fall forward. He simultaneously positioned his thumbs at the nape of her neck and moved them in a circular motion.

Chloe relinquished much of the tension of the

day thanks to Jack, but she discovered that it was quickly replaced by another sensation that could only be described as escalating awareness. She felt the impact of Jack's seductive touch right down to her toes. As she stood there, almost melting inside as pleasure rippled through her, she idly wondered how much longer her legs would support her.

"Better?" he asked.

"Much. Thank you."

"You're very welcome." His hands still atop her shoulders, he leaned down and pressed his lips to the side of her neck.

She trembled, the blood flowing through her veins suddenly turning hot and sluggish.

He slipped his arms around her and eased her back against his muscular body. His very aroused, muscular body.

Unable to stop herself, she relaxed against him. He tightened his encircling arms around her midriff. Her body responded to his closeness and the desire flooding her senses. Her breasts swelled in anticipation of his touch and her nipples tightened, as though inviting his mouth.

Chloe exhaled raggedly, but she didn't resist the feelings and urges swirling around inside her. Neither did she feel compelled to put space between them. If anything, she welcomed this reawakening of her senses and her sensuality. Needs and emotions, dormant since long before Martin's death, seethed within her now. They were both new and familiar. They were also a bit frightening.

She heard the shuddery quality of the breath Jack released. Chloe didn't say a word. She could barely breathe herself. Instead, she let herself feel. His warmth. His solidly constructed anatomy. His arousal.

"Should I apologize?" he finally asked.

She knew exactly what he meant. "Please don't."

"All right." He continued to hold her.

She basked in his strength. Closing her eyes, she rested her head against his shoulder.

"Eventful day," she eventually murmured.

Jack chuckled. "Might be a long night. You never know with little ones."

"Think we're up to the job?" Chloe asked. At a moment like this she felt as though they'd known each other forever. Perhaps even in another life.

"Definitely. Even if we weren't, he'd be worth the extra effort to come up to speed."

Chloe straightened, although she immediately missed their physical connection. She slowly turned in the circle of his arms.

He studied her as she peered up at him, his expression intent.

"I agree." She spoke from her heart, a heart that had been lonely for such a long time, a heart now filled with the pleasure of protecting and providing for an infant she already adored, a heart that still had room, she realized as she met his searching gaze, for the right man. Was he that man?

He bracketed her hips between his hands. "I'm really glad."

Quelling the urge to trace the width of his sensually shaped lips with her fingertips, she closed her hands into fists and rested them against his chest. Looking up at him, she said, "I know."

He smoothed his open palms up her arms. Once he reached her shoulders, he curved his hands over them. "Why does this feel so natural?"

"I'm not sure."

"Maybe we knew each other in another life."

"Maybe," Chloe whispered, startled because he'd voiced her whimsical thought of a few moments earlier.

He brought his hands up, his fingers sliding into the cloud of reddish-gold hair that framed her face, his thumbs against her temples. "So beautiful."

Still staring at his lips, she realized how much she longed for a taste of him, of his passion. She grappled with the hunger she felt, and she suddenly feared the strength of her need of him. She'd never wanted any man this much. What, she wondered, made Jack so different from the other men she'd met during her life? Why was the chemistry between them so vital?

"What are you thinking?" he asked.

Color flamed in her cheeks as she dragged her gaze up from his lips and refocused on him. She opened her hands and flattened them against his chest. The steady beating of his heart created a tattoo of sensation against her palms.

Smiling, Jack dropped a kiss on the tip of her

nose. "Me too." He paused, then asked, "Does that mean it's all right?"

She nodded, aware of what he intended to do.

"You make me dream," he whispered as he leaned down and took her lips in a searching kiss that rocked her entire world.

You make me want to believe in dreams.

She said the words in the privacy of her heart as she surrendered to Jack. She surrendered, as well, to the attraction already storming the crumbling barriers that surrounded her emotions.

He seduced her with his kiss, and then he made love to her with his lips and tongue as he delved into the heat and sweetness of her. He tantalized too. And he teased and taunted her in such a provocative manner that she wound up gasping for breath.

She felt shock resonate deep inside her. The shock of recognition. The shock of a soul-deep hunger that wouldn't be quenched until they became lovers. The shock of having her safe little world turned upside down by a man gifted with sensitivity and compassion for others even though she felt certain that he'd rarely been on the receiving end of such things.

She opened herself to him, giving him permission for complete access and demanding the same in return as she darted her tongue into his mouth and tangled it with his.

She felt his hands snug at her waist. She savored his strength. She inched closer, registering his hardness, then craving it, needing it, wanting it so much that she twisted against him. Jack made her ache in places that she'd learned over time to ignore. She couldn't do that any longer, Chloe realized. She probably wouldn't ever be able to do it again.

Despite her trepidation about trusting someone with her emotions, she was relieved to know that she could feel *and* desire a man again. Especially a man like Jack Howell.

His hands shifted suddenly, his fingertips gliding beneath the hem of her sweater. He left a trail of flame in his wake as he grazed her skin with his fingers and palms. When he finally brought his hands forward and cupped her breasts, she shuddered violently and moaned into his mouth.

She felt herself unraveling inside. She briefly worried about her sanity, because she wanted to pitch herself headfirst into the flash fire of their passion. She moaned once again, the sound rooted in the longing of her soul.

He drank in the sound as he smoothed his palms back and forth across her breasts, restrained by the sheer silk of her bra. He aroused her to a feverish state. And he evoked erotic mental images of their bodies joined in a quest for completion.

She arched when he plucked at her distended nipples, the sensations he caused streaming through her, overcoming her, reducing her world to feelings that were as complex as they were simple. Gripping his hips, she rubbed against him and heard his reaction in his harshly indrawn breath. She felt, too, the strength of his desire despite the fabric that separated them.

She wanted him. God, how she wanted him. She was shaking from the wanting inside of her.

He wrenched his mouth free and spoke her name. "Chloe . . ." She heard disbelief, need, and the torture of restraint. But then she heard another sound.

It confused her at first. When it finally registered, it brought her crashing back to reality. And it reminded her that they were standing in her kitchen and she was supposed to be preparing dinner.

In the end it was Jack who, without releasing her, reached out and switched off the kitchen stove timer.

Chloe felt like a drunk reeling from the effects of overindulgence. She also felt things she hadn't ever expected to feel again, and she very nearly wept at the realization that she'd been numbly going through the motions of life for more years than she cared to count.

Jack drew her close and simply held her. They both struggled for calm and balance.

Chloe suddenly remembered the garlic bread she'd put into the oven. Shifting free of Jack's encircling arms, she tugged her sweater into place, then lifted her hands and covered her face.

"Are you all right?" Jack managed, his voice low, raw.

She understood the pain she heard. She felt it too. Felt it right down to her soul. "I will be."

"Next week?" he asked.

"Next year," she predicted as she moved away from him—away from his warm, sturdy body, and away from the fantasies still spinning through her head.

Chloe pulled on the padded mitts she'd left on the counter beside the stove, opened the oven door, and removed a long foil-wrapped package.

"Garlic bread?" Jack asked, half-laughingly, half in disbelief.

She met his gaze after dropping the loaf on the counter, then nodded as she peeled off the mitts and shoved them into a nearby kitchen drawer.

"Did it survive us?"

She checked, her fingers clumsy as she peeled apart the foil to inspect the hot, garlic-and-butter-scented bread. "Yes."

"Will you?"

She smiled faintly, but she didn't speak. How could she explain all that she was feeling when she didn't completely understand it yet herself?

"I can't apologize."

Startled that he thought she expected an apology from him, she insisted, "I wouldn't want you to."

He closed his hands into fists and stayed where he was. She realized then that he wanted to touch her again, but that he was controlling himself. She appreciated his restraint, then she hated it. *I'm losing my mind*, she decided.

"I want you, Chloe McNeil. I hurt from wanting you."

She slowly turned to look at him. "Me too."

"I'm not used to feeling this way."

His candor made it impossible for her to be anything but honest in return. "Neither am I."

"What are we going to do?"

The bottom-line question. She knew the answer, of course, and she refused to pretend otherwise. "We're going to take care of Matthew."

He removed his glasses and placed them on the counter. "One day at a time?" he asked as he studied her.

She met his direct gaze. "Anything else is too soon."

He passed a shaking hand across his face, lowered his arm, and squared his shoulders. "Good plan." He moved out of her way as she returned to the sink.

She managed not to reach out and stop him as he crossed the kitchen. "It really is too soon for me, Jack. I don't want either one of us to make a mistake."

He nodded without looking at her before he walked to the wall of windows in the family room. As he stood there she stared at the bowl of lettuce in front of her. She wondered in the silence that followed what would happen next.

Some men, she knew, would have walked out the door already. Martin certainly would have. But what about Jack? Barely breathing, she waited and she prayed.

He didn't make her wait for more than a few

minutes. She risked a glance and saw him walk to the fireplace. Reaching for a log, he added it to the blaze he'd begun when they'd first arrived at her house.

When he turned to look at her, he smiled. She knew then that he wasn't going anywhere. The relief she felt almost drove her to her knees. It told her once again that he was a unique man. It also cracked her facade of composure.

After setting aside the dish towel she held, Chloe said in a tear-clogged voice, "I need to check on the baby."

She fled the kitchen a second later, tears streaming down her cheeks. She calmed herself as she stood beside the bed watching Matthew as he slept peacefully.

Once she reclaimed her wits and wiped away her tears, Chloe noticed that Jack had edged the perimeter of the dove-gray quilt atop her bed with pillows as a safety precaution. She smiled, whatever remained of her resistance to him crumbling to dust at this added evidence of his solid character and his ability to care about others. He wasn't even remotely like Martin, whose compulsion to control and manipulate had almost broken her spirit.

Bending down, she kissed Matthew's cheek and tucked his blanket more securely around him. She couldn't help envying him his peaceful slumber in a bed that had become the symbol of her one-person parade through life.

"Don't go there," she counseled herself as her thoughts turned to fantasies about what Jack would

be like as a lover. Determination marked her stride
as she slipped out of the bedroom.

Once she returned to the kitchen, Jack asked,
"Anything I can do to help?"

Chloe immediately noticed how much more relaxed he sounded. She knew that she was still a little
ragged around the proverbial edges, but she sensed
that Jack wouldn't push or crowd her. Glancing at
the bottle of wine and the crystal goblets she'd
placed on the kitchen counter a little while earlier,
she suggested, "Why don't we have a glass of wine
while I get everything ready to serve?"

Jack made short work of opening the bottle. After handing her a filled goblet, he leaned against the
edge of the counter and raised his glass in a toast.
"To new beginnings."

Smiling and growing more relaxed with every
passing second, Chloe echoed his words before taking a sip of the Chenin Blanc. "Spence and Viva are
partners in this winery."

"Spence mentioned that when he showed me the
wine cellar at their place."

"You'll probably receive a case or two as a housewarming gift. He's definitely into sharing the bounty
of his vineyard."

Jack laughed. "I'm counting on it."

"Have you seen them lately?" As she spoke
Chloe moved confidently around the kitchen, first
removing the pot of cooked pasta from the stove
top, then pouring it into a colander in the sink to
drain.

"I had breakfast with them this morning."

"They're very special people, aren't they?" she asked, her regard for the couple evident.

"That they are," Jack agreed.

"Viva told me you had a hard time believing that they sincerely wanted to welcome you into their family."

He nodded. "I was hesitant at first, having never had a real family, but I don't doubt their sincerity or their friendship any longer."

"You and Viva have a lot in common."

"Tommy told me about taking her in and giving her a home when her parents died. It was obvious that he thought of her as a daughter."

"Did you ever resent the fact that he was there for her but not for you?"

"For about five minutes," he answered with his usual candor. "But Tommy didn't know about me, so faulting him or begrudging Viva the stability he was able to offer her made no sense, in the final analysis. They weren't responsible for what happened to me. From what little I've been told about her, my birth mother was a very unstable woman."

"Do you remember her?"

"I don't have a mental image of her, if that's what you mean. I guess you could classify my memories as shadowy impressions, but that's about it." Jack paused, then admitted, "She left me with neighbors and disappeared when I was very young."

"I don't know what to say," she said, her heart aching for him. It made her appreciate her own family and the normalcy of her childhood that much more.

He mulled over her comment for a long moment. "There really isn't much to say. Once I worked my way through the anger I felt as an adolescent, I started to feel sorry for her."

"How did you avoid feeling sorry for yourself?" Chloe knew her questions were very personal, but she felt confident that Jack realized she wasn't indulging in idle curiosity. His past had helped to form his character, so it was relevant.

"I obviously didn't avoid it, any more than I avoided the anger that came from being abandoned. Everyone goes through a woe-is-me phase at one time or another in their lives, and I'm no exception. The turning point for me was when I was about fifteen or sixteen. I suddenly realized that she probably did me a huge favor." He shrugged. "I don't think I turned out too badly."

"You have a talent for understatement, Mr. Howell."

He chuckled. "You aren't the first person to make that observation," he confessed in a wry tone.

Chloe realized yet again just how much she liked Jack as a person. He could have become a bitter and resentful man. Instead, he'd fashioned himself into a man of integrity and honor. "Tommy must have been very proud of you."

Jack smiled shyly. "He said he was."

Chloe fought the urge to walk straight into his arms and embrace him. He'd known such loneliness and isolation, and yet he'd still wanted his late father's approval. Fortunately, he'd received it before Tommy's death.

Her smile was strained but genuine. "I didn't know Tommy very well, but I liked him. He had a generous heart."

Jack smiled then. Chloe was relieved, because she saw real pride in the man who'd fathered him in his facial expression.

"I don't think I've met anyone who didn't like him," he said. "My only regret is that we didn't have more time together."

"He was a father figure in this community. He was also a genuinely nice man." Chloe paused, then said, "So is his son."

He winced. "Ouch!"

Chloe grinned. "Nice is becoming a much-maligned word."

Laughing, he reached for his wine and took another drink of it.

"You are a very nice man, Jack Howell. Probably the nicest I've ever met."

"I'll take that as a compliment."

"Very wise of you, because that's how I intended it," Chloe assured him.

Jack wandered to the stove, where he paused.

"Thank you for answering my questions. I didn't do it to make you uncomfortable. For myself, I find that I sometimes resist dealing with the past, but when I do, it makes me feel better about the choices

I'm making for the future." She added dressing to the salad, tossed it, and set it aside.

"Ready for the sauce?" he asked.

"Please."

Using a pair of hot pads, Jack transferred the container of sauce to the tile counter beside the sink, then stepped back. "The only"—he paused, clearly searching for the right word—"discomfort I've ever felt around you is physical, so ask as many questions as you like."

Chloe smiled, her heart suddenly quite buoyant. "You get a hundred points for diplomatic phrasing."

Jack came up behind her, slid his arms around her, and hugged her. She savored the moment, just as she savored the sense of rightness she felt at being close to him. "I'm happy," she said very softly.

He lowered his head and pressed his lips to the sensitive skin at the side of her neck. "Me too."

Awash in a sea of sensation, Chloe struggled with her desire for Jack. She wanted nothing more at that moment than to make love with him, but she managed not to give in to the heated impulses threatening to overwhelm her common sense.

"I can wait, Chloe."

She exhaled, then nodded, grateful that he truly understood the conflict she felt. She couldn't speak, so she didn't try to.

Slipping out of his embrace, she placed Lucite tongs atop the tossed salad and set the bowl aside. She then transferred the drained penne into a large bowl, ladled a generous amount of marinara sauce over it, dusted the top with freshly grated Parmesan, and tucked a serving spoon into it.

Jack carried both serving bowls to the table. Carrying their wine, Chloe joined him. Jack pulled out her chair for her. Sitting down, she reached for her napkin and placed it in her lap.

Chloe finally met Jack's gaze. What she saw in his features made her respiration grow choppy and her heart stutter to a brief stop before it resumed beating again.

Chloe saw not only a reflection of the desire she felt, but she caught a glimpse of something more in his eyes. Something so far-reaching that she was reluctant to label it for fear she might be wrong.

As though aware of her mounting shock and disbelief, Jack calmly reached out to her.

Unable to stop herself, Chloe reached back. She slid her hand across his until their palms mated. She exhaled shakily, almost drowning in the heated intensity of his beautiful hazel eyes as they stared at each other.

In that instant Chloe embraced a knowledge she could no longer ignore. She was falling in love with Jack Howell.

EIGHT

Jack followed Chloe as she led the way out to the cottage shortly after midnight. He still didn't quite believe that she'd invited him to stay at her home while they cared for Matthew, but he refused to question this unexpected turn of events.

"The cottage used to be the cabana for the pool," she explained. "But it was wasted space nine months out of the year, so I turned it into guest quarters a few years ago."

Chloe had selected a burgundy-and-mauve color scheme for the interior. Decorated with sturdy wicker furnishings, the cottage was contemporary in design and the size of a large studio apartment.

Looking around, Jack took note of the kitchenette and eating area that lined the far wall. His gaze shifted to the double louvered doors that opened onto a spacious bathroom and an adjacent walk-in closet. The main room of the studio accommodated a king-size bed and an armoire, as well as a desk and chair and a pair of love seats positioned in front of an entertainment center that contained a television set, VCR, and CD player.

Once he completed his inspection, Jack smiled at Chloe. "All the comforts of home, and then some."

"I'm glad you like it."

He definitely liked the cottage. And he more than liked Chloe McNeil. He cared so much about her now that his emotions were all over the map and his heart was filled with hope. The kind of hope that he'd never allowed himself to feel before. He also liked the idea of being on-site to help with Matthew. He now connected happiness—real happiness—to Chloe. He'd seen it, of course, but he'd never truly experienced it.

The downside was obvious. Chloe presented a challenge to his self-control, but he judged the cost to his nerves a small one. He would simply have to adjust to being in a constant state of arousal.

Jack placed his large suitcase on the bed, then draped his garment bag over the top of it. He glanced out the window above the desk, which revealed the pinpoints of security lighting that circled the deck and swimming pool and separated the cottage from the main house. So close, and yet so far. The words were a cliché, he knew, but they'd never been more true.

"I think you'll be comfortable out here," she said.

When he heard the uncertainty in her voice, his

heart went out to her. "And I think you're being a very gracious hostess. I feel a little like the man in the stage play who came to dinner and then stayed."

She laughed. "There's an important difference. He wasn't invited for more than dinner. You were. Besides, you had to drive over to the hotel for your things," Chloe reminded him.

"A mere technicality." He approached her, his expression clouded with his concern for her as he reached out and clasped her hands. "Are you really sure about this, Chloe? I don't want you to feel pressured just because I'm staying here instead of at my hotel."

"I'm not totally sure of anything these days," she confessed. "I think I've said that before." She shook her head in obvious frustration with herself. "I always repeat myself when I'm tired. Anyway, nothing else really makes any sense. Matthew is much too small to be treated like a piece of luggage, so we can't very well cart him back and forth between your hotel suite and my house."

Jack squeezed her hands, still amazed by her invitation to use the guest house. She kept showing him sides of herself that intrigued and fascinated him. Her compassion for Matthew, her ability to accept the emotional price he knew they would probably both pay for taking the infant into their lives until his parents were found, the creativity that she didn't seem to recognize as unique, and her volatile sensuality.

In truth, her sensual nature had stunned him.

Jack had never known a more responsive or desirable woman than Chloe.

He realized, though, that the desire he felt for her had to remain under wraps for the time being. How, he wondered, was he supposed to accomplish that feat when things immediately went spinning out of control every time they got within touching distance?

Jack knew that Chloe was skittish and wary. He'd seen that kind of behavior in a lot of people over the years, and he recognized her hesitation as an understandable result of having been deeply hurt by someone she'd trusted. He hoped that she would find the strength to trust him and his feelings for her. He also hoped that he wasn't deluding himself.

Still, he wanted Chloe, wanted her in the same way that he wanted oxygen to breathe, but he wanted her as more than a lover. She personified everything he'd ever dreamed of in a life partner, but he suspected that such an announcement would send her fleeing to the nearest sanctuary, so he kept his emotions in check. It was difficult. More difficult than he'd ever imagined it might be to contain his feelings. He no longer minded, though, that fate had made him wait so long to discover the right woman—the woman his soul had longed for all of his adult life.

She slipped her hands free of his hold. "I've come to the conclusion that what we have here is a joint venture. It's perfectly logical for you to stay in the cottage, despite the tongues that will probably start wagging by midday tomorrow. And the schedule we've worked out is also logical."

"I'm always in favor of logic," Jack said, amused by her attempt to be so matter-of-fact about a potentially seductive situation.

"I'm glad."

Jack didn't miss the frown that suddenly marred her features. He watched her cross the room, pause in front of the armoire, and pull open the bottom drawer.

Once she pushed it closed again, she turned to look at Jack. "There are extra linens in here, so feel free to use them."

"Thank you." He smiled inwardly as she played her role as the skilled hostess.

She paused, then nibbled on her lower lip.

"Problem?"

"No, but I think I'll check on Matthew."

"He was asleep when we looked in on him five minutes ago."

"I need to check him, just to be sure."

"Want some company?" he asked as he watched her make her way to the door of the cottage.

She stumbled to a stop in the doorway and turned to meet his gaze. "What I want is to stop babbling. I must sound absolutely certifiable."

Jack shook his head, a gentle smile lifting the edges of his lips. "You sound tired, so get some sleep, Ms. McNeil. You've had a long day. I'd offer to tuck you in, but I don't think I'd be able to stop there."

Flushing, Chloe nodded her agreement. "Sleep well, Jack."

"You too."

She studied him, then said, "Matthew needs both of us." She groaned. "How many times have I said that today?"

Jack didn't care how redundant she thought she sounded. He understood that her words pointed toward a much larger issue—the emotional crossroads their relationship had led them to. "I know that Matthew needs us," he assured her, "but he's just a part of a bigger picture from where I'm standing, Chloe. A much bigger picture."

She hesitated briefly, then murmured, "Very true." Stepping backward, she tugged the door closed.

Jack exhaled, relieved by her acknowledgment of what was happening between them. Sheer force of will kept him from going after her. Muttering a word he rarely used, he ruthlessly smothered the hunger he felt for her. He walked to the bed, collected his luggage, and carried it to the walk-in closet.

As he unpacked his things he told himself that he possessed the strength of character not to impose his needs or desires on Chloe. He also repeated what now reminded him of a mantra: Chloe wasn't ready for intimacy. He sensed that she viewed it as a commitment. To commit, especially from her vantage point, equaled a pledge of trust. She was close, he suspected, but she wasn't there yet, and he refused to be guilty of rushing her.

He fell asleep almost immediately after stripping off his clothes and taking a warm shower. He awoke at dawn, his body so taut with sexual tension that he groaned. It took all of his self-control not to throw on a robe and make his way to Chloe's bed.

Instead, he brewed a pot of coffee, put on a pair of sweats, found his moccasins, and went in search of the morning paper. He walked out to the circular driveway in front of the house just as the paperboy hurled the paper from his moving pickup truck.

Jack grimaced as he strolled along the path to the rear of the house, concerned that he'd probably set in motion the wagging tongues that Chloe had mentioned the night before. He let himself into the house via the patio, checked on Matthew, who was still asleep, quelled the urge to look in on Chloe, and returned to the cottage for coffee and the morning paper.

He reentered the main house about an hour later. He found Chloe in the kitchen. Cradling Matthew in her arms as she fed him, she glanced at Jack as he approached her. She smiled a smile that reminded him of a brilliant summer sun, the kind of smile that assured him that she was her confident, poised self once again.

Once they worked out a few kinks, the routine they established that first day served them well in the week that followed. Chloe went to the office each morning, leaving Matthew in Jack's care. Once she returned at lunchtime, he used the afternoons to deal with his obligations.

They shared most of their meals, all of their evenings, and their delight over Matthew. They took turns cooking, and Chloe discovered that Jack not only appreciated good food, he was quite capable of making it in the kitchen. They enjoyed companionable silences, late-night conversations, and frequent laughter-filled moments.

All the while they both constantly struggled to deal with the escalating awareness they both felt.

An unspoken bond of trust developed between them, despite their smoldering attraction to each other. Chloe realized that, instead of demanding accountability from her or trying to control her every move as Martin had done, Jack respected her as an individual. As a result, she relaxed a little more with each passing day.

His steady nature, nonjudgmental attitude, good humor, and patience heightened her confidence in herself and solidified her feelings for him. Although Chloe remained uncertain about Jack's feelings for her, she no longer doubted his sincerity. His behavior reinforced, time and time again, her belief in his innate decency.

Matthew, remarkably well behaved most of the time, did what all babies have done since the beginning of time. He basked in the love given to him by the two people responsible for his well-being.

Decorating Fairhaven continued on schedule. They took Matthew with them to the various showrooms. Armed with Jack's seal of approval on the design style to be used in the mansion, Chloe requested rush shipments on the draperies, floor coverings, and furniture for the mansion. She hoped that the suppliers would honor their commitment to deliver everything the week before Christmas.

As Jack revealed additional details about his past, Chloe gained a more complete picture of him as a man. She also fell more deeply in love with him. He confided in her about the isolation and transiency of undercover work for the Justice Department. Although he didn't complain, the loneliness that he'd endured throughout his life was quite evident.

When he spoke at length about Tommy Conrad and the assignment that had brought them into contact, she saw the love and respect he felt for the man who'd fathered him, even though they'd discovered each other late in Tommy's life. she realized that, instead of having his ability to express his emotions blunted, Jack possessed the capacity to give unstintingly to those he cared about. Chloe found inspiration and the courage to overcome her own restraint in his emotional generosity.

Their second week as a threesome unfolded in much the same way as their first week. Viva and Spence dropped in for a visit following a dinner party they'd attended at a neighbor's home.

Although Chloe maintained her commitments to her current clients, she decided against taking on any new ones for the time being. For the most part, she, Jack, and Matthew remained undisturbed by the world. Chloe mentally blessed Sheriff Sturgis for protecting their privacy. He telephoned each morning with updates on his search for Matthew's parents, and he dropped by whenever he was in the neighborhood. Articles about the abandoned infant appeared regularly in both local and regional newspapers, and the television stations displayed his photograph several times a day. Offers to adopt him poured in, but no one claimed him as their own.

Chloe dreaded the very idea of giving him up, but she tried not to dwell on the inevitable. Even though he didn't say much, she knew that Jack shared her anxiety. How could he not? Matthew meant the world to both of them.

Seated in the rocking chair in the nursery with Matthew cradled in her arms, Chloe heard a floorboard creak. She glanced in the direction of the sound and saw exactly what she expected to see— Jack standing in the doorway of the room. His presence didn't surprise her. He often started his day before dawn, and it was in his nature to be very alert to the activity that took place in the main house.

Chloe pushed up from the chair, careful not to disturb Matthew's slumber. She carried the infant to the bassinet and gently placed him in it. After drawing the covers up to his shoulders, she leaned down, kissed the back of his head, and then made her way out of the nursery.

After checking the intercom to make sure that it was turned on, she shut the door before she spoke to Jack. "He was hungry, so I decided to feed him. He's adopted your early-bird-gets-the-worm mentality, I'm afraid."

"I guess I'm a bad influence," Jack said with an easy smile as they walked down the hallway. "I noticed the light was on in your bedroom when I got up. I thought something might be wrong."

"Nothing's wrong." Chloe paused in front of the open doorway to her bedroom. "Matthew made it very clear that he wanted a clean diaper and a full stomach, in that exact order."

Jack chuckled. "Ah, the simple life."

Leaning against the door frame, Chloe grinned. "No kidding."

"What about you?"

She felt the heated sweep of his gaze as they stood facing each other. Her pulse picked up speed as she thought about the way he tasted. She longed for another taste. Desire coiled like an overwound spring deep inside her body, and the blood rushing through her veins scalded her senses.

Chloe bit back the moan hovering on the tip of her tongue, and she fought the impulse to pitch herself directly into Jack's arms. She felt restless and edgy. In truth, she'd felt that way for days, but she didn't want to admit it to Jack. Neither did she plan to confess that sleep had become an elusive goal for her. She slept in exhausted snatches, the desire she felt repeatedly jarring her into wakefulness hour after hour, night after night.

Their togetherness was, she realized, a double-edged sword. They were a great team for Matthew and she adored their time together, but the constant strain of not giving in to the desire that crackled like electricity between them was wearing Chloe to a frazzle.

Jack cupped her cheek with the palm of his hand. "What about you, Chloe?"

She blinked, then refocused on his face. She saw how puzzled he looked and told herself to snap out of it. "What about me?" she quipped.

"You okay?"

"I'm awake." She couldn't think of anything else to say.

Jack chuckled as he looked her up and down. "I can vouch for that. Want a glass of juice or some coffee?" he asked.

"I'm fine, but you go ahead."

"You're sure?"

She sighed, feeling oddly deflated, then nodded.

"Talk to me," Jack pressed in a low voice.

She brought her fingertips to her temple and pressed the pulse throbbing there. "I can't sleep."

Jack drew her hand away from her face and lightly kissed her knuckles. He didn't release her hand but kept it clasped loosely in his own.

Chloe got the impression that he wanted to say something significant, but that he didn't want to say the wrong thing. This was one time, she realized, that she didn't want him to be such a gentleman.

"Sleeping peacefully is a major challenge, isn't it?"

She nodded, assured by his tone of voice that they were finally on the same conversational page. "You haven't kissed me in a long time. Why?" Looking up at him, she waited for an answer.

Jack frowned. "It's a little early in the day for this conversation, isn't it?"

"Not really, unless you don't want to answer my question."

"I think the answer is obvious."

"It's not," she said.

"I wouldn't want to stop with a kiss."

"And I wouldn't want you to."

"What exactly are you saying?" Jack asked, his eyes narrowed and filled with countless unasked questions.

She turned her head and pressed a kiss into the center of his palm. "I'm saying that I know why I can't sleep."

"You're worried about something?" His voice suddenly sounded ragged.

"That's pretty accurate, but for the sake of clarity, I think this is a good time to come right out and admit that I don't want to be alone in my bed any longer. I'm worried that you're going to stay away." She waited then, wondering how he would respond to her bluntness. When he didn't say anything, she summoned what remained of her nerve. "Have I made you uncomfortable?"

Jack closed the space that separated them. "Profoundly, but I'm not complaining." He curved his hands over her shoulders.

She trembled, the silk of her nightgown doing nothing to deflect the heat of his touch. "Then what are you, if you aren't uncomfortable?" Shifting forward as she spoke, she looped her arms around his waist. She settled against him, sighing shakily as the warmth of his sturdy body sent heat and awareness of his masculinity all the way to the marrow of her bones.

He encompassed her with his embrace. She willingly molded herself to him. She felt the shudder that ripped through him a heartbeat later. Her eyes fell closed, and she submerged herself in the sensations caused by the ridge of engorged flesh that pressed against her lower abdomen.

Shaking with desire, she opened her eyes and tilted her head back so that she could see his face. All the while she savored the sturdiness of his very muscular, very male anatomy. An image of the two of them making love flashed across her mind, and a shiver of anticipation traveled the length of her body a few seconds later.

"You're shaking."

Chloe nodded. "I've missed you."

"I've been here," he tenderly reminded her.

"But you've only touched me when we were caring for Matthew. That's a different kind of touching."

"What kind of touching do you want?" he asked.

She thought for a long moment about how to answer him. In the end she settled for the admission, "Your kind of touching. I dream about what it will be like."

"Tell me, Chloe," he urged after he leaned down and kissed her so deeply and so thoroughly that she grew dangerously dizzy. "Give me specifics, so I'll know our dreams are the same."

She felt heat suffuse her body, felt as well the tightening of her nipples. The hard points of flesh became so sensitive that she wanted his mouth on them. Sucking. Gently teething. She wanted to absorb him into her pores and bask in his seductive essence. She wanted to surrender to his passion, surrender so totally that it wouldn't matter where she ended and he began.

"I want to be naked, and I want your hands on me." The utter eroticism of her admission caught her off guard. Who had she become? When had she ever been willing to give up the control she exerted over herself and her corner of the world? She knew the answer. Not ever. Not until Jack Howell.

"What about my mouth?" he asked as he shifted his hands to her breasts, cupped their weight, and tugged at her nipples. "Do you want my mouth on you, Chloe? Do you want those feelings too?"

Sensations collided within her and then exploded

like tiny starbursts in a night sky. She gasped. "Oh, yes. I want it all, and then I want more."

"Everywhere? Do you want me to use my tongue and my lips and my fingers to explore every inch of you? Do you want me to know you that well?"

Her eyes widened and her breath caught in her throat, the images he created with his questions almost too much to bear. No one but Jack had the power to seduce her with words.

"Tell me, Chloe," he pressed as he leaned down and licked the tip of each breast through the silk covering her.

Feeling slightly dazed, she watched him straighten. "I want you to touch me everywhere," she whispered. Her body, particularly that secret place at the top of her thighs, started to throb as she imagined the intimacy they would soon experience. "I want to feel you inside me. I want to share everything possible with you."

His sex surged against her lower abdomen. She shimmied closer, hating the clothing that separated their bodies. She slipped her hands between their bodies and stroked his jeans-covered groin with an upward motion of her fingertips. He shuddered and threw back his head, but he kept plucking at the distended tips of her breasts until she felt like screaming her pleasure.

"I've waited . . . we've waited . . . long enough. It's time," she breathed, not recognizing the rawness of her own voice, but understanding for the first time that primitive impulses served to empower lovers.

"I didn't want to pressure you."

"You haven't, Jack."

"You're sure?" He moved his hands downward, dragging his knuckles across her skin until he reached her waist.

She wanted to bring his hands back to her aching breasts, but she contained the impulse. "I've never been more sure of anything in my life."

"Without promises or guarantees?" he asked. "Do you need them in order to feel safe, Chloe, or can you trust me now?"

His questions made her hesitate, but only briefly. She realized that she would take whatever risks were required of her and pay any price to experience Jack as a lover.

She trusted Jack, with her heart and her life. And she loved him, even if he didn't know the truth. She sensed his respect for her, and she knew that he both liked and desired her. What she didn't know was if his feelings for her went any deeper than liking. She wasn't about to ask, though.

In the privacy of her heart Chloe hoped that Jack was falling in love with her, but she didn't consider love a requisite for intimacy between them. As for commitment, it was a separate issue. She didn't want to deal with it now. She just wanted Jack, wanted him so much that she could feel her body grow- ing more and more aroused, so aroused that she trembled as they studied each other in the semidarkness of the hallway.

"You haven't answered my question," he said as he gripped her waist and pressed her against his powerful body.

She felt every inch of his desire for her. As she twisted and turned against him Chloe also reached up and traced the width of his lower lip with a single fingertip. "I love the way you taste."

Jack smiled, a lazily seductive smile that made Chloe's heart race. Breathing unevenly, she traced backward along the seam of his lips with the tip of the same finger.

He exhaled, bathing her skin in damp heat. She didn't take her finger away. She simply looked at him, her pulse points pounding wildly, the temperature of her body steadily climbing.

Jack parted his lips and sucked on the fleshy tip of her finger. She breathed shallowly in the seconds that followed, her imagination filling her mind with images too erotic for words. Sucking the digit a little farther into his mouth, he used his tongue to wet her skin. Another part of her body began to soften and moisten in anticipation.

Thoroughly shaken, Chloe's thoughts scattered like a covey of startled birds. She moaned very softly.

Jack pressed an intimate, openmouthed kiss into the center of her palm. She curved her hand against the side of his face, the rasp of his beard adding to the sensations already suffusing her senses.

"I'm still waiting for an answer, Chloe," he reminded her.

She smiled, loving the low gritty sound of his voice as he spoke. He was hungry for her, as hungry as she was for him, she realized.

She brought her fingers to the buttons at the front of her floor-length silk nightgown. Her gaze on Jack's shadowed features, she released all one dozen buttons without breaking eye contact.

"Is this my answer?" he asked as he smoothed aside her gown with hands that shook.

She nodded, then stood motionless as he pushed the white silk gown free of her shoulders. She felt it skim the length of her shapely body before it puddled around her feet and ankles. Chloe listened to Jack mutter a word that would have sounded crude under any other circumstances, but she heard wonder and reverence in it.

He claimed her lips and covered her breasts with possessive hands. She clung to him as he alternated between massaging her aching flesh and tugging at her taut nipples. She felt overwhelmed by his sensual assault, so overwhelmed that her knees threatened to buckle.

Jack wrenched his mouth free a short while later. "You're exquisite," he managed raggedly.

She shivered, then swayed unsteadily.

He swung her up and into his arms. She sighed with relief as he carried her into the room and settled her in the center of the bed. Sprawled on her back, she watched him strip off his jeans and T-shirt.

He was more physically fit than she'd imagined. She openly admired the muscular symmetry of his body as he lowered himself onto the bed and drew her into his arms.

She knew she'd never wanted or needed anyone more, but that knowledge no longer frightened her. Thanks in large part to Jack's patience during the preceding weeks, she felt the strength of a simple truth. She wanted to give herself to the person she loved.

As Jack took her lips and staked his sensual claim on her, Chloe experienced the certainty that this was the right time in her life to express her love for the man who'd captured her heart.

NINE

Jack took his time with Chloe. He didn't want to rush her, despite the need seething within his own body. Whatever the cost to himself, he was willing to pay it in order to assure her pleasure.

Although he still felt thrown off balance by the honesty of her desire for him, he worried that she might feel regret later. His worry strengthened his determination to put her needs first.

As they reclined on their sides facing each other, he gave in to the love he felt for her and let himself pretend that she loved him in return. He allowed himself the illusion of being loved for a simple reason—he wanted any intimacy that they shared to be based on more than physical desire.

As he embraced Chloe, Jack basked in the myriad sensations caused by her hard-nippled, full breasts pressed against his chest and the welcoming, cradling width of her hips. His maleness was trapped between them. With every subtle uptilting of her hips as she rocked against him, Jack experienced a heated surge of response in his loins. He ached in every cell of his body for fruition.

As he held her and explored the sweetness of her mouth, he stroked her trembling form from shoulders to hip, over and over again, until he knew every line and curve of her torso. He felt her hands moving in concert across his shoulders and down the length of his spine. She left incendiary little bursts of sensation in the wake of her skimming fingertips.

Without relinquishing her mouth, he shifted her onto her back in one smooth motion, the weight of his upper body supported by his muscular arms. His insides clenched, and his musculature tremored as he began to settle between her parted thighs.

He fought the temptation to take her then, even though she reached out to touch him intimately. He felt the glide of her fingers as she caressed him. His heart trembled with shock and his body threatened to detonate.

Breathing shallowly, he found the self-control that was an essential part of his personality and quelled the urge to drive into her depths once and for all. As much as he longed to satisfy the need that had throbbed unceasingly in his body since their first moments together, he drew her hands away from his maleness, kissed both palms, and then sank carefully down atop her.

He positioned himself at the gateway to her body, letting her feel the pulsating power of his arousal. He didn't seek more. When she gripped his hips with both hands, tried to wriggle closer, and then sighed her frustration into his mouth as he kissed her, his restraint very nearly crumbled.

Jack freed her lips a short while later, his breathing choppy as he lifted his head and looked down at Chloe. She opened her eyes and met his gaze, a smile as alluring as any he'd ever viewed curving her lips.

"Hi there." His voice resembled a stretch of gravel road as he gathered her close and nuzzled the fragrant curve of her neck.

"Hi there, yourself." Reaching up, she framed his face between her hands.

"We can stop anytime, if that's what you need. All you have to do is give me a signal of some kind."

"What's the signal to proceed on course?" she asked, her bright green eyes sparkling with mischief.

He adored this side of her. "I hadn't given it much thought."

She tugged his head down, sucked his lower lip between her teeth, and worried the expanse of flesh for more than a minute. When she released him, she asked, "Does that work for you?"

Her unwillingness to deny her appetite for him made his heart trip violently in his chest. "That'll definitely work."

"I'm glad." Searching his features, she looped her arms around his broad shoulders. "I can't imagine wanting to stop. Not ever."

He closed his eyes, inhaled, and then exhaled raggedly. Relief made his heart swell.

"Problem?" she asked, using his shortened version of the question.

He smiled once he refocused on her. "You're a tease."

Chloe laughed. "No one's ever said that to me before. Be careful, or I might think I'm the next Mata Hari."

"You could seduce me from a distance of a thousand miles, Ms. McNeil."

"Amazing."

She really looked amazed, and he realized that she didn't have a clue about her impact on him. "It happens every time I hear your voice."

"A simple phone call would turn you on?" As she spoke she kneaded his hips with her fingertips and experimentally rocked her pelvis.

He sucked in a sharp breath. She reminded him of a seductive jungle feline. "Only from you," he confirmed.

"I think I like that. We'll have to try it out and see if it actually works."

"How about later?" he gritted out between clenched teeth. "I'm a little preoccupied at the moment."

As though to prove his point, he shifted down her body and lowered his head. Cupping her breasts with both hands, he sucked a nipple between his teeth and tortured it with his swirling tongue.

Chloe groaned, and her back arched.

Jack sucked more aggressively, drawing her deeply into his mouth. He felt her dig her fingers into his hips, but the scoring effect of her fingernails simply heightened his desire for her and made blood surge hotly into his groin.

Chloe groaned yet again when he used his teeth on her sensitive nipples. She clutched his head with both hands, and the soft, gasping sounds that passed her lips were unlike anything he'd ever heard before.

So aroused that he hurt, Jack paused. "Was that a yes?"

"Yes." The word emerged as a tortured sound. She drew in enough air to feed her need for oxygen, then whispered, "I can feel you. I want you inside me."

Need jolted through his loins like heat lightning. "Too soon." He wanted nothing more than to join their bodies, but he refused to go quickly this first time. He returned to her taut nipples, captivated by the sensitivity of the mauve peaks. He intended to savor her and what they were sharing, even if it killed him.

"Not too soon," she insisted, writhing beneath the erotic torment of his suckling mouth and the rhythmic kneading of his fingers as he fondled her breasts.

He shifted slightly. "Much too soon," he told her in that rough tone of voice that spoke to the tenuousness of his restraint.

He traced a path from the deep valley between her breasts, down her midriff, and then across her quivering stomach with the tip of his tongue. He painted her skin with searing strokes, anointing her body in such a way that she shook beneath his hands and mouth. The gasping sounds that she made spurred him on.

He didn't stop until he was kneeling between her ankles. He applied his lips to the delicate arch of her left foot, then trailed his tongue up across her inner ankle and along the shapely curve of her calf. He felt the muscle flex just seconds before a shudder passed through her.

He moved on, his touch like a scorching brand as he leisurely created a path of kisses up the inside of her thigh. Despite the seductively silky feel of skin that smelled like spiced vanilla, he rerouted his sensual expedition before he risked falling victim to the enticing heart of her femininity.

Switching his attention to her other leg, he traced a pattern of wet heat along her inner thigh, over her knee, and down to the curve of her calf. He paused only after pressing a last kiss to the arch of her right foot.

Straightening once again to a kneeling position, Jack studied Chloe as he tamed the impulses storming his own body. She visibly trembled in response to his sensual foray.

He changed tactics, abandoning much of the restraint he'd shown until now. Drawing her across the mattress so that her hips were even with the edge of the bed, he brought her legs up and over his shoulders as he knelt on the floor. He tucked his broad-palmed hands beneath her buttocks, bent forward, and placed his mouth over her.

Chloe jerked with shock, but she didn't pull away. Gripping the bedding with both hands, she turned pliant as a willow as Jack claimed her musky sweetness for himself. He used his lips and tongue to make that claim.

He lavished every bit of the skill he possessed as a lover on her, her complete seduction his ultimate goal. She trembled, then moaned low in her throat as he flattened his tongue against her delicate flesh. Treating her like the ultimate delicacy that she was, he indulged himself, alternating between stabbing forays and lingering licks of her quivering femininity. She tasted like heaven, her essence a powerful aphrodisiac to Jack's senses.

He added yet another dimension to the sensations she was already feeling by tucking two narrow fingers inside her. Chloe stiffened briefly, her muscles tremoring around his fingers. Her moans turned into breathless cries of disbelief a few moments later. She bucked beneath him.

He relentlessly pursued his quest for her satisfaction, easily controlling and guiding her to climax. He didn't cease until she started to come apart in the safety and security of the loving vise formed by his mouth and hands.

Chloe gasped, then came up off the bed and clutched at Jack's shoulders as her release imploded deep within her body. She cried his name, and his heart soared at the shocked pleasure he heard in the sound. He continued to love her, but with the kind of gentleness rooted in love.

Chloe slowly descended from the peak of her release. "Jack, please," she whispered, sounding tearful as she reached out to him with both hands.

Alarmed by the emotion in her voice, Jack moved back onto the bed. He sat beside her. As he smoothed his hand up the length of her still-trembling body, his anxiety eased when he saw in her expressive face nothing more complex than her desire for him. He drew her up, positioning her astride his muscular thighs. With his hands at her waist, he sank back into a half-reclining position courtesy of the mound of pillows at the head of the bed.

Chloe shifted forward and sprawled across his broad chest, twining her arms around his neck in the process. She sighed heavily, the sound replete with relief. "That's better."

He smiled, despite his desire to plunge his aching flesh into the recesses of her body and remain embedded within her forever. "I'm glad you approve."

She straightened up, settling more securely atop his thighs as she inspected his features. "I approve. You surprised me. You're so . . . talented."

He chuckled, easing up from the pillows so that they faced each other. Sliding his palms up her arms, he shuddered when he felt her shift against him. Her tight nipples nudged through the hair that covered his chest and imprinted his skin with points of heat.

"Would you rather I wasn't?" he asked, his voice sounding ragged thanks to the sensations rioting through him.

She pursed her lips, considering his question for a long moment before she answered. "Nope."

"Good."

"Better than good," she remarked. "There aren't enough superlatives to cover how you made me feel."

He inclined his head, male pride visible in his hazel gaze and the almost smug look on his face. "I'm glad."

She grinned almost playfully. "Me too."

She tucked her hand between their bodies, then combed her slender fingers through the dense thatch of coarse dark hair that encircled his manhood. His chin lifted, and his eyes fell closed for a moment. He exhaled raggedly. Tension and anticipation tightened every muscle in his body.

"Careful," he muttered as he smoothed her long legs around his waist.

"I have to touch you," she announced as she dragged her knuckles up his rock-hard belly and then down again.

His heart galloped, and his respiration grew shallow. Jack studied her through narrowed eyes, then cautioned, "There are consequences."

She gave him an impertinent look, and said in an equally impertinent tone of voice, "I certainly hope so."

Jack laughed at her comment, but his laughter

quickly turned to a low growl of pleasure when Chloe clasped him securely between her palms. He saw the challenge in her gaze, so he gave in to the pleasure flooding his senses instead of trying to deflect her touch. As she tantalized him with her stroking fingers his blood ran so hot that he felt in danger of going up in flames.

Jack needed Chloe's hands on him. He needed her touch almost as much as he longed for her love. She was volatile and responsive, passionate and uninhibited, sensual and thoroughly seductive. She embodied everything he'd ever craved in a lover, and then some.

Jack dropped a hard little kiss on her lips. "I want your hands on me. I also want to bury myself inside your body."

She scooted forward in response to his erotic confession, but he stopped her before she could impale herself with his jutting sex. She exhaled in a huff and glared at him.

She opened her mouth to speak, but Jack claimed her lips and brought his hands to her breasts. As he covered them and gently squeezed the full globes, he felt her nipples pucker and stab at the palms of his hands.

Because he denied her what she wanted, Chloe improvised. She cupped the fragile area beneath his maleness with one hand and used the other to clasp the base of his arousal. Leaning forward, she peppered his neck with stinging little kisses before she shifted backward and looked at him.

Jack watched her then, a muscle ticking high in his jaw and his nostrils flaring ever so slightly when she pressed the head of his sex against the sensitive flesh between her thighs.

He drew in a steadying breath when he felt the wet heat of her. He felt as well the way she quivered with response each time she stroked herself with his manhood. He swelled to near bursting as she stoked the flames that burned with corresponding intensity within both of their bodies in the minutes that followed.

He gripped her waist, not aware that he risked leaving fingerprint bruises on her fair skin. Unable to restrain himself, he jerked her forward, driving into her in one powerful thrust.

She gasped with surprise, then made a sound that reminded Jack of a purr. In danger of exploding, he held her still until he regained some semblance of control.

Chloe clung to his shoulders as he slumped back against the mound of pillows, shifted into a kneeling position astride him without breaking their connection, and then slowly sank down until Jack was fully encased in her body.

"So perfect," she moaned as she moved with increasing confidence.

He covered her breasts with his hands and plucked at her tight nipples as her body seemed to ebb and flow with his. "You're perfect."

She shivered, her back arching as he aroused her with skillful fingers. Head thrown back and eyes closed, she smiled as she rode him with her senses engaged and her awareness of anything but the two of them completely gone.

Jack surrendered to the consuming sensuality of their lovemaking. He penetrated her depths with forceful upward thrusts, and he savored every twisting downward movement of her pelvis as she met his passion with her own intense need.

He stopped fighting the inevitable soon after. He embraced it instead, but only after Chloe found her release. Her body quaked and tremored around him with such force that he went spinning out of control and into a sensation-filled oblivion that stunned him with its sustained force.

His emotions went the way of his body, and in an instant of clarity he knew that his life would remain incomplete if Chloe wasn't a part of it.

Shudders racked him in the aftermath of the almost excruciating pleasure of his climax. Chloe eventually collapsed across his chest in an exhausted, breathless sprawl. Jack clasped her to his broad chest, his heart racing and his breathing still erratic.

Feeling restless and on edge, Chloe paced back and forth in front of the formal living-room window. She paused briefly every few minutes and peered outside, but she saw nothing other than the dense foliage that edged the rolling, snow-dusted hills and the winding driveway of the acreage she'd called home for many years.

Chloe disliked waiting for anything, especially when she feared it might be bad news, but a telephone call from Sheriff Sturgis a little while earlier had left her with no other alternative. Lost in thought, she flinched when Jack placed his hand on her shoulder. She turned and met his gaze. As they studied each other she saw his worry in the frown that furrowed his brow.

"Try to relax," he urged.

"I can't," she admitted, glancing down at Matthew, who slept peacefully in his arms.

Extending her hand, she traced the curve of his cheek with her fingertip. Her chin wobbled and her heart lurched painfully in her chest. She slowly withdrew her hand, and she reminded herself of a lesson that she'd learned long ago—life was changeable and happiness was often fleeting.

After repositioning the baby, Jack slid his free arm around Chloe and pulled her against him. Sighing, she allowed herself the luxury of leaning her head against his shoulder for a few minutes.

So much had changed in such a short space of time, she reflected. She'd begun to feel that the intimacy they'd shared a few hours earlier had happened to two other people. Instead of being able to savor and celebrate this new chapter in their relationship, they were both tense and worried thanks to the message they'd found from Sheriff Sturgis on Chloe's answering machine.

His remark—"We need to talk to you and Jack about the baby, so Lisa and I will arrive at your place around noon"—had sent a chill across her heart. She still felt cold inside, because she knew that the possibility of Matthew being placed in someone else's care was a very real one.

Too nervous to remain still, Chloe shrugged free of Jack's encircling arm and stepped away from him. She resumed her pacing, although she remained alert to Jack and the baby with every step she took.

His expression remote, Jack strolled in the direction of the fireplace on the far side of the formal living room. Matthew did his usual thing. He wrinkled his nose, blew a few bubbles, and then smiled in his sleep.

Chloe watched the two as she wore a path in the carpet. She resented feeling afraid and helpless, but that was precisely how she felt. The feelings reminded her of her past and the emotional uncertainty of her life with Martin.

"What if they take him?" she asked.

He met her gaze, but he didn't answer her.

"Do you think they will?" she pressed, her reference to the sheriff and Lisa Hampton, the Social Services coordinator for their area of the county.

"I don't want to speculate, Chloe. It's a possibility, of course, but let's not borrow trouble."

"Everything's been so perfect. Matthew is safe and happy with us, and I . . . ." Her voice trailed off. *I'm happier than I've ever been in my life*, she realized, *but I've been kidding myself.*

She felt like a fool for pretending that they were a family, but she hadn't been able to help herself.

She'd fallen in love with both Jack and little Matthew, and she loathed the very idea of losing either one of them.

"If the sheriff's found his parents, then we have to let him go."

"How can you sound so calm?" she burst out.

Matthew stiffened in Jack's arms at the sound of agitation in Chloe's voice. The infant frowned, but he settled down as soon as Jack rocked him. Rather than express any annoyance with her, Jack gave Chloe a compassionate look.

She realized that he felt as awful as she did. She brought her fingertips to her temples, took a calming breath, and then pressed her hands together. "Sorry. I must sound like an idiot right now."

"You sound worried, so there's no need to apologize. I don't want to lose him, either."

"If they've found his mother, won't there be a court hearing of some kind to determine her fitness as a parent?"

"That's what usually happens."

"I want only the best for Matthew, Jack. I know I'm biased, but I really believe that we're what's best for him."

"If you're looking for an argument, you're not going to get one from me."

She smiled wryly. "I really wasn't expecting one."

"Do that again, why don't you?" Jack suggested.

"Do what?" she asked.

"Smile for me."

She did, but ever so faintly.

"This morning was nothing short of amazing," he said, his tone of voice so intimate that she ached all over again for his touch. "*You* are amazing."

"And you, sir, are too talented for words."

"I'm glad you weren't disappointed."

"Not possible, Jackson Howell. Not even remotely possible."

"I'm glad," he said. "And I'm glad we have each other."

Chloe fell silent. Her smile faded and her worry reasserted itself in her thoughts. Would they lose Matthew today? Dear God, she hoped not.

Gravel crunched. She glanced out the window and saw the vehicle that pulled up her driveway. "They're here," she whispered.

She watched Sheriff Sturgis and Lisa Hampton, a lovely and very capable social worker in her late twenties, exit the patrol car. Her gaze didn't leave them as they made their way up the flagstone path that led to the front door of her home.

Jack stayed near the warm fireplace and gently rocked the still-sleeping infant. Chloe reluctantly approached the front door. She pulled it open before the chime sounded, a gust of cold air preceding Lisa and the sheriff.

Stepping aside, Chloe motioned them inside. "Let me take your coats," she offered quietly.

"It's lovely to see you again, Chloe." Lisa Hampton's Alabama roots were evident in her soft voice. She shrugged out of her coat. "It's been months since we've had a chance to get caught up on each other's lives," she commented.

Chloe nodded and managed a strained smile before she put their heavy coats in the hall closet. "I've made a pot of coffee. Would either of you like a cup?"

"I don't care for anything, but thanks for asking," Lisa said.

Bill Sturgis rubbed his hands together to ward off the chill caused by the low outdoor temperature. "Sounds good to me. It's cold out there. According to the weather service, we're due for a heavy snowfall tonight. The odds are pretty good that we'll have a white Christmas."

Jack joined them in the foyer after Chloe closed the front door. Once Bill took care of the introductions, Lisa immediately shifted her attention to the bundle in Jack's arms.

"Why don't we go into the family room?" he suggested.

Chloe led the way. Jack handed Matthew to her after Lisa and the sheriff sat down on the sofa. Jack made himself comfortable beside Chloe on the love seat opposite them.

Chloe glanced at Matthew, who was sucking on his fist as he slept. Tears stung her eyes as she looked at him, but she blinked them away before she met Lisa's gaze.

"He's a beautiful baby," the young woman remarked.

Chloe nodded, the emotion wedged in her throat

preventing her from speaking until she swallowed a few times. "He's perfect."

Jack met her gaze as Chloe glanced at him. She found courage in his reassuring smile and the feel of his arm around her waist.

"Have you found his parents?" Chloe asked, unable to tolerate the unknown any longer.

Bill shook his head. "Unfortunately, no. After two weeks of nothing but offers to adopt him, I'm coming to the conclusion that we've got a real dilemma on our hands. No one seems willing to step forward with the truth. We're going to have to make some decisions about this young man's short-term future as a result."

"How are you coping as foster parents?" Lisa asked.

"Very well, although we had a little adjusting to do at first. Matthew lets us know what he wants or needs most of the time," Jack answered. "We improvise the rest of the time."

Chloe thought he sounded like a proud father. She knew in her heart that he would be an extraordinary father when he had his own children. Casting a sidelong glance in his direction, she couldn't help wondering if they would ever experience that pleasure together. In a perfect world, Chloe concluded. Only in a perfect world.

"Most new parents do a great deal of improvising, so it sounds as though you're on track." Lisa smiled at them. "He's obviously a good baby. When I spoke to Dr. Hansen this morning, he provided me with the medical data I need for my case file on Matthew. My impression is that he's in excellent health."

Chloe nodded. "We take him to the clinic every week for a checkup just to be sure."

Lisa's smile widened. "I wish everyone took their responsibilities as seriously as you two. It would make my job a lot easier. Will you give me a tour of the nursery?"

Chloe pushed to her feet, the baby still cradled in her arms. "Certainly."

As the two women walked out of the family room, Jack heard Chloe ask, "Would you like to hold Matthew?" He relaxed then, certain that she had also sensed that Lisa Hampton was there to help the baby, not jeopardize his well-being.

TEN

Bill looked at Jack, his expression troubled. "She's getting mighty attached to the boy, isn't she?"

Jack didn't try to deny the obvious. "We both are."

"It's hard not to, especially for someone like Chloe. She's strong, but Martin wasn't an easy man to live with." He shook his head. "He never really appreciated her, and he kept her from having the things in a marriage a woman usually wants."

He understood what the sheriff meant, despite his attempt to be tactful. Jack had already concluded that the man had been a selfish creature. Denying Chloe children had been just one of his sins in their ill-fated marriage. "I've gotten that impression from Viva and Spence."

"I'm still worried she'll take it hard when the parents show up."

Jack chewed on his lower lip for a moment.

"Whatever happens, we'll deal with it together," he said.

"I kind of thought you'd feel that way." Bill Sturgis took a drink of his coffee. "My boys might be full of the devil some of the time, but I wouldn't trade any one of them for all the money in Fort Knox. Although it'll probably cost me a fortune to send them all to college." He chuckled. "I may need to get a second job."

Jack smiled. "I used scholarships and the GI Bill for most of my education."

"Trust me, Amanda and I are always talking up good grades and scholarships to our brood."

Jack asked, "No red flags from the FBI, the state police, or the National Center for Missing and Exploited Children?"

"Not a one, which is why I keep thinking his parents are local teenagers. They'll probably come forward, but it'll take a while. Are you both still willing to do this thing day by day?" Bill asked.

Jack nodded. "Of course."

"Just making sure."

"We want what's best for him, Bill."

Sturgis studied Jack. "You had a rough go of it as a kid, didn't you?"

Although surprised by his question, Jack didn't try to sidestep it. "It was lonely."

"I'd hate to think of my boys going through their lives without knowing their momma and me. You must have been one tough little guy."

Jack smiled, remembering the black eyes he'd given and received. "I survived."

"You did a hell of a lot more than survive, Jack. I admire your grit. I imagine Tommy did too." The sheriff smoothly changed the subject in the next breath. "You do much fishing when you lived up north?"

Jack smiled at the *up north* part of the sheriff's question. "In Virginia, as a matter of fact. Fresh and saltwater both. How about you?"

Bill nodded. "There's a place not far from here by the name of Lake Sterling. In the spring, why don't we take my boys and make a day of it?"

Once again, Jack realized, he was being welcomed into his late father's community. He felt warmed by the sheriff's gesture of friendship. "Thank you. I'd like that."

"Good. We'll do it, then." Bill Sturgis finished the last of his coffee and placed the mug on the coffee table in front of him. "The media's been real cooperative. It's been a nice change of pace from the way they usually operate."

"I've seen the newspaper and television coverage," Jack remarked. "From what you said last week, I gather you've already canvassed most of the hospitals and clinics in the county."

The sheriff nodded. "I've also circulated copies of the picture I took that first day at Doc Hansen's, and the word's out to all the law-enforcement agencies in Kentucky and the surrounding states, but I haven't got so much as one solid lead about the boy."

Jack dealt with his most immediate concern when he commented, "From what I know about the system, Miss Hampton may have to place him in a home certified for infant care."

"I don't think she's decided anything yet. She just got back yesterday from her trip. Lisa's not prone to leaping to conclusions about a situation. She tends to mull things over. It helps that she also has a lot of discretion, since her bosses in Louisville expect her to work with the local community, not against it. Pretty enlightened way of doing business for a government agency, if you think about it," Sturgis added.

As Jack nodded his agreement the two women returned from their inspection of the nursery. Both were smiling while Matthew gurgled happily in Lisa's arms. Jack was relieved to see Chloe's relaxed demeanor, and he gave the social worker credit for putting her at ease. Once Lisa returned Matthew to Chloe, she took her seat on the couch, reached for her briefcase, and extracted a clipboard and several printed forms.

"Everything in order?" Jack asked as Chloe sat down beside him.

Lisa smiled. "Completely. You two have been very thorough. I also like the intercom system that's in place in the house." Her gaze traveled between the two for a long moment. "I don't usually make snap decisions about anything, but I think I'm going to change my MO today."

Bill chuckled. "Lisa's husband is an investigator with the county prosecutor's office."

Jack nodded while Chloe lifted Matthew and placed him against her shoulder when he started fussing. He immediately quieted as she gently rubbed his back.

"We've got some work ahead of us if we're going to get you two on the certification roster. Shall we get started?"

Sounding like the lawyer that he was, Jack asked, "Will you give us the larger picture, Mrs. Hampton, just so we're certain of your meaning?"

"Call me Lisa, please. And the larger picture is as follows: I've known Chloe for several years, and I can speak to her good character. So can most of the people in this community. As far as I'm concerned, she more than qualifies as a foster parent." Lisa paused, then focused directly on Jack, her expression quite serious. "I've also spoken to the Justice Department, Dr. Hansen, and to Spence and Viva Hammond about you, Jack. You more than qualify, as well. It's quite clear to me that you've both gone to a great deal of trouble, probably disrupted your own lives in the bargain, in order to guarantee that Matthew is properly cared for. You've more than demonstrated your credibility and your stability. Matthew is thriving in your care, and I feel it would be an error in judgment on my part to uproot him at the present time."

Matthew grunted and waved his arms. Chloe laughed softly, Bill grinned, and Lisa smiled indulgently.

"I think he approves," Jack remarked, much of his tension departing.

"I'm certain you're right," Lisa agreed. "What I'd like to do is get the paperwork started." She tapped the stack of forms attached to her clipboard. "By getting you into the application pipeline, I can temporarily certify you, and that certification will be immediate. There's no way of knowing how long it will take for Matthew's natural parents to step forward, so we're involved in a waiting game of sorts. That's hard on everyone, but being foster parents provides you with legal standing. I'm confident that you, as an attorney, understand how convoluted the legal process is when we're dealing with an abandoned infant, but I also believe that you're in a position to be effective advocates for Matthew if the need arises."

"I'm impressed," Jack confessed.

"I'm relieved," Chloe added.

Matthew made a chirping sound, thus adding his two cents' worth and bringing smiles to the faces of everyone in the room.

Circling Chloe's shoulders with his arm, Jack smiled at her. He saw hope and relief shining in her eyes. He shared her feelings, but he was particularly glad that her anxiety about the baby had diminished. He felt confident that they were doing the right thing, for Matthew and for themselves.

If anyone had ever told him that an abandoned infant was destined to play a major role in his life, Jack would have declared it ridiculous. Now, though, he knew that anything could happen.

He'd fallen in love with a remarkable woman, and they were being given the opportunity to provide for a child that no one seemed willing to claim. Jack promised himself that they would do what was best for the little boy. He was honest enough to admit to himself that by giving time and love to Matthew, he was letting go of some of the pain from his own childhood.

Several hours later, after eating lunch, filling out a mountain of Social Services forms, and putting Matthew down for a nap, Chloe donned a heavy jacket and accompanied Lisa and Bill out to his patrol car. She expected Jack to join them once he completed a phone call with his contractor for Fairhaven.

Bill answered his cell phone as they reached the car, his booming voice sounding authoritative as he spoke. Given his tone, Chloe assumed he was speaking to one of his deputies at the sheriff's station in town.

After depositing her purse and briefcase in the backseat of the patrol car, Lisa faced Chloe. "I like your Jackson Howell a lot."

"He's not mine."

Lisa's surprise showed in her animated features. "Take a closer look," she advised. "That is one terrific man. He reminds me a lot of his father."

"He still looks startled when people say that to him," Chloe confided.

"It's no wonder, Chloe, given the circumstances of his childhood. Did you know all the details?"

"No, I didn't. When he was answering your background questions, I couldn't help thinking how easily he could have wound up on the wrong side of the law."

"Truer words were never spoken. You wouldn't believe some of the situations I've tripped over in the Social Services system. As I said, Jack Howell is one terrific man. He'd be the kind of husband you've always deserved."

Chloe sighed. "We haven't known each other very long," she said, still somewhat uncertain about her ability to make a long-term commitment to any man, no matter how much she might love him. She reminded herself yet again that Martin and Jack were as different as night and day, and she needed to remember that fact.

"I knew immediately that Ted and I were right for each other. So did he." Lisa studied Chloe for a long minute while Bill Sturgis kept on barking orders into his cell phone. "You and Jack would make great parents. It's also pretty obvious you two love each other, so why don't you think about marriage and making some babies of your own?"

Chloe's jaw dropped, and her eyes widened.

Lisa grinned at her. "Didn't know I was such an impulsive little soul, did you?"

"You've definitely gotten my attention," Chloe admitted.

"Ted and I had a thirty-day courtship," Lisa told her. "Our families were pretty stunned, but we knew we were meant to be together, so we talked to our minister right away and arranged to exchange our vows. Life's too short to put happiness on hold."

"We're not in love with each other, Lisa. It would be silly to pretend we are."

Lisa gave her a quick hug, then stepped back, a gentle smile on her face. "He's not Martin, so don't be afraid of what your heart's trying to tell you." She pulled open the door on the passenger side of the vehicle. "Let's get together soon and have lunch. I've missed seeing you."

Although still reeling from Lisa's advice, Chloe nodded. "I'd love to. Why don't I call you on Friday and we'll set a date?"

Bill finished his cell-phone conversation just as Lisa took her seat in the car. Chloe watched him lift his arm and wave in the direction of the house. "I'll be in touch," Bill called out.

Turning, Chloe watched Jack make his way down the flagstone path to the driveway. She couldn't help noticing his somber facial expression, although he gave Bill a thumbs-up gesture to acknowledge the man's remark. Jack paused at her side, but he didn't say anything or reach for her hand. They stood together in silence as the patrol car pulled away.

Puzzled, she asked, "Is everything all right with Matthew?"

"He's fine." Jack finally met her gaze. "How about a snack?"

She smiled, although something about his expression nagged at her. "My appetite is back, so you're on. What are you fixing?"

He half smiled. "Anything you want."

She arched an eyebrow. "Are you on the menu?"

He shook his head, his smile broadening to a full-fledged grin. "I think that can be arranged."

"Good, then I want you for dessert." She gave him a pert look, turned, and started up the walkway to the front door. She skidded to a stop when he seized the back of her jacket. "Yes?" she asked, dragging the word out for as long as her breath lasted.

He laughed once he turned her around and they stood toe-to-toe. "You're amazing."

"You've said that before." Feeling playful thanks to the success of the morning, Chloe slipped her arms around his waist and nuzzled his neck with her lips. "I guess I'll have to believe you, won't I?"

"Do that," he suggested, his hands stealing under her jacket. He smoothed them up the front of her body and made a discovery that darkened his hazel eyes to a deep chocolate.

Leaning back so that she could see his wonderful angular face, Chloe smiled. "Surprised?"

"Where you're concerned, I'm learning not to be." He reversed course, slid his hands beneath the hem of her cropped sweater, and then up and over her breasts. The fact that she hadn't bothered with a bra that morning was all the encouragement he needed. He closed his hands over her taut-nippled breasts, a ragged-sounding sigh escaping him.

Chloe moaned very softly as Jack caressed her full breasts. As he leaned down and slanted his mouth over hers, she mentally congratulated herself for lightening his mood and then surrendered to her hunger for him.

She still didn't understand what had caused his somberness a few minutes earlier, but she refrained from asking for an explanation. Chloe rationalized that their concern for Matthew and the hectic morning with Lisa and Bill had been tough on both of them. Jack had every right to react to the stress they'd experienced.

The snowflakes drifting down from the pewter clouds bunched up in the midday sky eventually drove them indoors, but only after they shared several deep kisses.

They succeeded in reigniting the desire that had flared between them during the predawn hours. While Matthew enjoyed his noontime nap Chloe and Jack turned their backs on the cares and concerns of the world and indulged their passion for each other.

In the days that followed, Chloe noticed that Jack often seemed preoccupied, but he insisted that nothing was amiss. She finally concluded that he would speak up if he had something important to say.

She realized that Jack Howell might be viewed as reserved by people who didn't know him well, but with Chloe he wasn't shy about expressing himself or his needs. She knew that he wasn't using his quiet time to manipulate her, because Martin had used that tactic so much, she easily recognized it.

While Social Services processed their application as infant foster-care providers, the threesome moved forward as a makeshift family, despite all of the uncertainty of their situation. Matthew thrived and constantly delighted them, Chloe dealt with her clients courtesy of an abbreviated schedule, and Jack prepared his lecture notes for his first semester teaching pre-law and worked in tandem with Chloe, sharing household tasks and caring for Matthew.

Their nights were filled with the kind of intimacy and sensuality that Chloe savored. Jack's skill and generosity as a lover astounded her. He took her to heights she'd never experienced before. Whether tender or volatile, their lovemaking began the final stage of a healing process she hadn't even realized she needed. He inspired her to express her deeply sensual nature with an openness denied to her during her marriage.

She fell more deeply in love with Jack each day, but her feelings were a mixed blessing. A part of her wanted to shout her love for him from the rooftops. Another small part of her still wondered if love eventually meant a repeat of the domination and control that had destroyed her first marriage. In fairness to Jack, she credited him with never attempting to undermine her.

Although she pondered the pros and cons of a committed relationship with Jack during private moments, she never let herself forget a very important fact. Jack expressed his desire for her and his admiration of the life she'd created for herself in a hundred different ways, but he never spoke of love.

I love you. Three very simple but terribly complicated words that Chloe longed to say to Jack, but she didn't. Humiliating herself and making him uncomfortable with declarations of love weren't on her list of things to do.

The furnishings for Fairhaven started to arrive from the various manufacturers about ten days before Christmas. Clad in old jeans and warm sweaters, with Matthew snug and gurgling happily, or snoozing, in a large blanket-lined woven basket, Chloe and Jack met each delivery van at the mansion. They shared the task of directing the placement of rugs, window coverings, and furniture with ease.

As they strolled through the first floor of the house to inspect the results of several days' work, Jack slipped his arm around her and dropped a kiss on her forehead. "You've done a great job, Ms. McNeil. I'm in your debt."

She glanced up at him, uneasiness stealing into

her heart. "I'm glad you approve." Why, she wondered, did his words remind her of a dismissal?

"I definitely approve. Visualizing the way you want a place to look in your mind is one thing, but having someone understand the concept and then make it happen for you is something else altogether." He eased free of her at the entrance to the library and strolled into the center of the room.

Chloe remained in the arched entryway, hating the burst of insecurity that suddenly threatened to overcome her. She struggled not to reveal her distress by smiling at Jack. Her smile felt stuck, though, and almost painful, but she held on to it and her pride with both hands.

She knew she'd done her best for him, so why did she feel so sad? The answer to her question was all around her. They'd been playing house and playing at being a family, but that would soon end, she realized.

"I'm going to enjoy living here, Chloe, and I owe it all to you."

"Tommy gave you Fairhaven," she reminded him softly, "so I can only take credit for doing my job as a decorator."

"You've done more than you realize. I finally have a home, and that means more to me than I can say."

Tucking his hands into the pockets of his trousers, Jack gazed around the spacious library once more. The lush fabrics draping the windows and the antique Aubusson carpets covering sections of the restored hardwood flooring, as well as the oversized leather club chairs and couch, were masculine and sturdy.

Although she wanted to share in his pleasure and bask in his praise, Chloe ached inside as she watched Jack. She'd created a remarkable environment, an elegant home for the man she loved, a home that he would soon occupy—but not with her.

Chloe heard a cry of distress from Matthew, and the sound jerked her from her melancholy thoughts. "I'll be right back," she choked out, grateful for a reprieve from her pretend smile.

Turning, she hurried down the hall to the formal living room, where he'd slept in his basket for almost an hour. She comforted Matthew. She also derived comfort from him as she held him and whispered soothing words of love and reassurance to him.

His cries diminished as she cradled him close to her heart, gently rocked him, and allowed herself to weep for the sense of impending loss she felt. As her tears slowly abated Chloe wandered in the direction of the windows that overlooked the rose garden on the north side of the house.

As she stood there she fought for control over her emotions. She heard the sound of Jack's footsteps a few minutes later. Hastily wiping away her tears, she squared her shoulders and managed a watery smile for Matthew, whose little face silently peered up at her with what could only be described as a curious look. His lower lip trembled, as if the uncertainty of Chloe's emotional state worried him.

"It's all right, sweetie," she whispered as she dropped a kiss on his chin and smiled at him.

"How's he doing?" Jack asked as he came up behind her and slipped his arm around her shoulders.

Chloe didn't look up. Keeping her head bowed, she exhaled shallowly before she spoke. "He's fine. I think he must have had a bad dream."

Jack fell silent. Chloe held her breath, aware of how damp her voice must have sounded.

He released Chloe and moved to stand in front of her. Tucking two fingers beneath her chin, he lifted her face into view. "Talk to me," he urged quietly.

"What about?"

"You've been crying."

"Don't be silly," she protested. "I must have gotten something in my eye when we were shifting the furniture around. There's enough dust in this place from the packing supplies to choke an elephant."

Jack frowned, certain she was lying to him. Why, though? he wondered. And what had her upset enough for tears?

"I think you've been working too hard," he announced. What he wanted to say, he didn't. He wanted to tell her he loved her, loved her more than life itself, but he managed to contain the impulse. He didn't intend to run the risk of scaring her off with premature statements about the depth of his feelings for her.

She still seemed skittish and unsure of herself,

and he wanted to wait until she'd rebuilt her confidence before he expressed his feelings. He wondered, though, if he'd somehow misread the situation. Was he doing them both a disservice by being patient and pursuing a waiting game? He didn't know the answer, but he knew he needed to figure it out fairly soon. The stress was making him crazy.

Shrugging, Chloe ducked her head and studied the baby. "Maybe, but a little work won't hurt me, so quit worrying."

"I do worry about you, Chloe," he said. "Why wouldn't I? You're juggling a hell of a lot right now, and I'm responsible for most of it."

"I'm an adult, Jack, and I've learned my limits over the years, so give me some credit for knowing where to draw the line and when to take a break."

"Credit given," he conceded. "But I think we both need a break, so we're going to have one in the very near future."

She lifted her face into view, her expression somewhat bemused. "What kind of break?"

"That's a surprise. Friday night? Say around six?"

"Are you asking me out on a date?"

"Yeah, and I could kick myself for not doing it sooner."

She laughed, but the sound was suspiciously soggy. "I wouldn't want you to bruise your anatomy on my account."

He reached out and cupped her cheek with the

palm of his hand. "I'd do just about anything to make sure that you know how much I appreciate you."

Turning her head, she pressed a kiss into his palm. Her eyes fell closed, and she exhaled shakily.

Still worried, Jack gathered Chloe and Matthew into a gentle embrace. He basked in the sense of rightness he felt as he held them both, and he couldn't help wondering what it would take for Chloe to fall in love with him.

A voice in his head cautioned him to be realistic. She didn't love him, and she didn't realize that he'd fallen in love with her.

Was his love enough to sustain them, Jack wondered, or would they be destined for failure if he proposed marriage on the strength of his feelings for her?

ELEVEN

"Did you forget something when we were here this morning?" Chloe asked when Jack turned off the main road and guided his car up the long driveway at Fairhaven on Friday evening.

He cast a quick glance at her, the relaxed smile on his face concealing the conflict he felt. "I wanted your opinion of a framed print that arrived this afternoon. A friend in Washington shipped it to me as a housewarming gift. I thought we could take a look at it before dinner."

Chloe smiled, then shrugged. "I'm just along for the ride." She settled back in the passenger seat, her gaze on the rolling, snow-covered hills that were part of Jack's property.

"You're in a sassy mood, aren't you?"

"Of course, I am. Matthew's with Viva and Spence, so I know he's well cared for, Anne and Tom Shelby are happy with the work being done on their bed-and-breakfast inn, I'm wearing a new dress, and I'm out with my favorite guy. All in all, I'd say that life is nice."

Jack reached out, took her hand, and brought it to his lips. He pressed a kiss to her knuckles, then held her hand until they reached the circular driveway in front of the mansion.

As he turned off the engine and pushed open his car door, Jack noted that the caterer had followed his instructions to the letter. He'd parked his van out of sight and dimmed the lights in the front rooms of the mansion at the designated time.

Jack assisted Chloe from the passenger side of the vehicle. Both dressed in semiformal attire, they made their way to the double front doors of the mansion. Jack used a remote device to shut off the security system and release the lock before ushering Chloe through the doors and into the foyer.

When she reached for the light switch, he caught her hand before she could flip it on, tugged her into his arms, and kissed her. His senses registered the hourglass shape of her body as he embraced her. Jack smothered the groan rising up inside of him as she melted against him.

She revealed her hunger for him without hesitation, her lips parting and her tongue darting into his mouth to duel sensually with his. She slid her hands beneath his suit jacket, her fingers tracing around his narrow waist, then smoothing up his back. He relished her responsiveness, so much so that he lingered at her mouth and sampled the passion of the woman who would possess his heart until he drew his final breath.

Jack reluctantly lifted his head and looked down at her. Her lips, so lush and inviting, made him want to throw caution to the wind and carry her upstairs to the master suite. But he didn't. Too much needed to happen, and too many plans had already been made to change course now. He wondered how she would react to the real purpose of their evening together.

Lifting her hand, Chloe curved her palm against the side of his face. "You do that very well, Mr. Howell." Her eyes twinkled.

"Shall I do it again?" he asked.

Her stomach growled. She laughed. "I really think food should come first. I haven't eaten since breakfast."

"Your wish is my command."

"Thank you, kind sir." Chloe whisked her thumb across his lower lip to remove a streak of lipstick before she lowered her hand. "Back to normal. Now, let's have a look at the framed print your friend sent."

Jack took her hand, led her across the foyer and down the hallway. He paused a few steps before they reached the arched entryway to the library. "Close your eyes, please."

Chloe gave him a curious look. "You're serious?"

He nodded.

"That print must be a one of a kind," she remarked as she closed her big green eyes and waited.

"Keep them closed until I tell you to open them."

"Yes, sir, Mr. Howell." She saluted.

"Nice touch, Ms. McNeil."

She laughed softly, but her eyes remained closed.

Still holding her hand, Jack guided her forward until they stood at the entrance to the library. Scanning the room, he made sure that everything was in order before he slipped behind Chloe, tugged her back against him, and circled her waist with his arms. He leaned down, kissed the side of her neck, and then straightened.

"Jack? What's going on?"

"Why are you whispering?" he asked, his eyes sweeping over the decorated Christmas tree—all eighteen feet of it—positioned on the opposite side of the spacious library. His gaze shifted to the fireplace. He nodded to the man standing beside it, then waited while he put a match to the kindling beneath a stack of logs, replaced the mesh safety screen, and darted out of the room.

"I don't know why I'm whispering," she admitted. She sniffed delicately. "Something smells good. Almost like pine trees in the forest."

"I thought we'd have a fire while we were here."

"When can I open my peepers?" she asked.

Jack smiled at her impatience. "Now would be a good time, I think."

"You're sure?" she asked.

"I'm sure."

She opened her eyes. "Oh, Jack, how beautiful!" she exclaimed.

He tried to view the room from her perspective, but what he saw was something unique as far as he was concerned. This was the first Christmas tree he'd ever had in a home that he considered his own. He knew that it would only be a real home, the perfect home, if Chloe decided to share it with him. He prayed that she would as he gazed at the towering Scotch pine, which was covered with crystal ornaments, festive garlands, and glowing lights.

Viva and Spence had helped him decorate the tree that afternoon while the caterer from Louisville had taken over the kitchen. A blazing fire in the fireplace and a table for two, set with the finest crystal, silver, and china, completed the preparations for their evening. Lighted tapers had been positioned in the center of the linen-covered table. The chef and his two uniformed waiters stepped into view.

Chloe turned in Jack's arms, tears shining in her eyes. "You did all this for us?"

He heard the wonder in her voice, and he promised himself that he would always take time to show her how much he truly appreciated her. If she allowed him that luxury, he silently amended.

He smiled, then dropped a hard little kiss on her parted lips. "I did it for you, Chloe, because you deserve all the good things that life has to offer."

"No one's ever . . . I mean . . . it's wonderful, Jack," she finally managed, her composure shaken. "Thank you so much."

"You're very welcome." He grinned down at her. "I should be the one thanking you, though."

Chloe gave him a puzzled look. "Why?"

"You do so much. I can't keep track of it all most of the time, so I don't even know where to start."

Her stomach growled a second time. She laughed. "Food would be a good place to start, I suspect."

"Then let's feed you, because there are other things on our agenda this evening."

"Do tell," Chloe remarked as they entered the library.

"Later," Jack promised, taking her arm and guiding her to the table.

She paused while he drew out her chair. "Promise?"

"You don't like surprises?"

"I love surprises, but the suspense is tough on the nerves," she confessed as she sat down at the table for two.

Once he took his seat, Jack watched her slowly scan the room. She grew even more wide-eyed as she studied the exquisitely decorated tree and the wrapped gifts piled high beneath it. He loved the almost childlike delight he saw in her animated features.

Chloe refocused on Jack. "I'm totally dazzled."

"Be patient," Jack counseled, extending his hand to the center of the small table.

Chloe reached out so that their palms touched.

"Does that mean you're going to dazzle me even more?"

He smiled, then squeezed her fingers before releasing her hand. "Possibly."

"Then I definitely need nourishment," she announced as she sank back in her chair.

The waiters stepped forward, took their napkins and shook them out, and placed them in their laps.

Thus began a leisurely dining experience with perfectly prepared and graciously served courses along with the finest wines from Spence's California winery.

Without being the least bit intrusive, the waiters attended to all of their needs during the next hour and a half. The chef and his staff discreetly departed at the conclusion of the meal. The only thing they left behind was a silver tray that contained a crystal dish filled with strawberries dipped in white chocolate, two linen napkins, a carafe of coffee, cups and saucers, and a decanter of cognac and two snifters.

Sharing the love seat that gave them a perfect view of both the roaring fire and the glowing Christmas tree, Chloe and Jack enjoyed their privacy. They passed a snifter of cognac back and forth while they chatted.

"How do you feel?" Jack asked after he took the snifter and set it on the end table beside the love seat.

Chloe didn't answer his question right away. She snuggled closer, though. "Content."

He chuckled. "Perfect word. Perfect evening."

He kissed her forehead, then her lips. She tasted of strawberries and white chocolate.

"More dessert?" she asked, a flush filling her cheeks.

Jack drew her from his side and onto his lap. He felt the seductive press of her shapely bottom against his thighs. The muscles in his body thrummed in response to the heat flooding his loins. "Are you available?"

She grinned. "With or without chocolate?"

He arched an eyebrow. "Whatever makes you happy."

"Shall I do what makes me happy?" Chloe asked.

"By all means," Jack encouraged, his pulse picking up speed because he'd seen this side of her before. He sensed something different about Chloe tonight, though. There seemed to be a touch of recklessness in her, and it intrigued him. It also aroused him. "If there's anything I can do, be sure to let me know."

"I definitely think that there are things you'll want to do," she commented before she slipped off his lap, kicked off her high heels, and turned to stand before him.

Jack didn't say a word. He simply watched, his admiration of her delicate beauty and innate sensuality sending streaks of heated awareness into his bloodstream. She was the most remarkable and diverse woman he'd ever known. And the most desirable.

"Did you decide yet about the chocolate?" Chloe

asked, her hands gliding up the front of her dress. Her gaze on his face, she smoothed her open palms across her breasts. Her nipples beaded beneath the silk fabric.

Jack swallowed, the air in his lungs burning, begging for release.

She touched the button at her throat with a fingertip.

Chloe paused, an expectant look on her face. Lips slightly parted, she moistened them with the tip of her tongue as she waited for him to answer.

His heart stuttered to a stop in his chest, then resumed beating. As it picked up speed again his gaze swept down the line of tiny buttons that graced one side of the front of her floor-length, Chinese-style silk dress. He didn't stop until he reached her silk-covered legs, which were revealed by two strategically designed slits in the fabric.

The dress fit her like a second skin. He knew then what she was about to do.

"I've decided," he answered, his voice almost too low to hear. "I want you. I guess I'm a purist, since nothing else appeals to me."

She smiled. "I thought I'd try my hand at dazzling you."

"I definitely like the sound of that." He removed his glasses and placed them on the end table beside the brandy snifter.

As he loosened the knot of his tie and then tugged the length of silk free, Jack tracked the slow movement of her fingers as she released the buttons that held her dress together. She started with the one at her throat. Drawing in a breath, then exhaling shallowly, she worked her way past her waist and over the flaring width of her left hip. Bending forward, she released the last of the buttons, the final one at the top of the slit that revealed the seemingly endless length of her shapely leg.

Jack reminded himself to breathe as she slowly straightened and looked at him.

"Can you help me?" Chloe whispered, taking a step forward. She paused between his muscular thighs.

His loins throbbed, threatening his control. His body felt incendiary as he shifted forward on the cushions. He watched her face as he reached out and peeled her silk dress away from her body. Her eyelids fluttered closed, her thick auburn lashes like mink fans on her high cheekbones.

Chloe lifted her shoulders in a slight shrug. A moment later her dress whispered down the length of her body and puddled at her ankles, exposing her high full breasts with their taut mauve peaks.

Jack bit back the groan that the sight of her caused.

Naked except for a pair of skimpy panties and thigh-high silk stockings, Chloe opened her arms to him. Her breasts swayed ever so slightly as she adjusted her footing. "I'm glad you're a purist," she said, the words spoken in an erotic whisper that scorched his senses.

Jack responded to her summons, shifting forward

even as he savored her seductive instincts. She inched closer—close enough for his breath to cause her nipples to bead even more tightly. He saw the invitation in her facial expression, and he responded by cupping her breasts with his wide-palmed hands and pressing his lips against the valley between them. He inhaled the vanilla scent of her skin, and was seduced once again.

Chloe shuddered delicately, then clutched at his shoulders. Seated on the edge of the love-seat cushions, Jack licked first one and then the other nipple. Chloe moaned out his name.

Jack sucked one of the hard tips into his mouth and teethed it. He tantalized her, flooding her senses with sensations so far-reaching that her knees threatened to buckle. She dug her fingers into his shoulders when he shifted to the other nipple and sensitized it with the same intense dedication.

He slid his hands down to her hips and cupped her buttocks. Edging his fingers beneath the silk panties she wore, he slipped them free of her hips, down her thighs, and allowed them to join her dress. He alternated between painting the undersides of her breasts with lazy strokes of his tongue and sucking at her nipples until he heard Chloe whimper. The sound was too need-filled to ignore.

He ran his hands up the insides of her thighs, then combed his fingers through the silk covering her feminine secrets. Chloe groaned, the sound long and low, almost like a plaintive plea. He tucked two narrow fingers into the wet heat of her body and felt her shudder.

He also felt the hot rain of her passion as he stroked her with his fingers. She jerked when he placed his thumb over the nub of flesh at the top of her sex. Utilizing every erotic skill he possessed, Jack drove her to the brink.

She unraveled suddenly, tiny internal convulsions tremoring around his clever fingers. She screamed his name as she climaxed, her lengthy release quaking through her body until she slumped forward and started to collapse.

Jack caught her before she could fall. Gathering her against his chest, he held her as she slowly descended from the summit of her release.

Chloe whispered his name. He heard shock and amazement in the sound. Gently lowering her to the cushions of the love seat, he stood, stepped out of his shoes, and hastily stripped off his clothing.

Chloe watched him disrobe through half-closed eyes. Her body slowly renewed itself, her senses reawakening and responding to the muscular definition of Jack's body. She went willingly into his arms when he reached for her, but he surprised her by drawing her off the love seat and urging her onto the tufted rug positioned in front of the fireplace.

Naked and sprawled on her back, Chloe reached up for him, but he deflected her hands.

"Are you warm enough?" Jack asked, reaching for some of the throw pillows on the love seat and tucking them beneath her head and shoulders.

She smiled, a smile reminiscent of the first Eve. "I'm on fire."

"Still?" he teased as he stretched out beside her and placed his hand on her hip.

She turned in to him, pushing at his chest with her hands until he cooperated and rolled onto his back. She positioned herself on her knees between his thighs. Her gaze traveled slowly from his proud arousal, across his muscle-ridged stomach, then higher to his broad, hair-roughened chest.

"Still," she confirmed, laughter and seduction in her voice as she met his gaze and rhythmically kneaded his sturdy thighs.

Jack fought for control. "I'm going to dazzle you again," Chloe said. With that announcement made, she leaned over him, clasped him between her hands, and took him into her mouth.

As her tongue glided over the head of his engorged shaft, Jack sucked in a sharp breath, then another. He heard the deafening roar of his own heartbeat, and he felt the searing rush of flame that spilled into his bloodstream. He shuddered, ready to explode. He started to pull free of her.

"Let me," Chloe whispered against his hard flesh, as if sensing his dwindling control. She paused briefly, although she stroked him lovingly with her fingers as she glanced up the length of his tremoring body. "Trust me."

Grinding his jaws together, Jack jerked a nod in her direction. He gripped handfuls of the rug beneath his trembling body.

She gave to him then, gave with a generosity that stunned his heart and devastated his senses. Chloe loved Jack with the combined power of her hands, lips, tongue, and teeth. She also made a gift of her heart. She told him that she loved him without saying a word, but there was eloquence in her statement despite the silence. She couldn't say the words yet, but she'd discovered the perfect way to express herself by sharing the ultimate intimacy with Jack.

This unique intimacy presented her love as a gift, and it was the only way she could give it for now. She hadn't found within herself the courage to admit her feelings for Jack aloud, although she searched daily for the strength she needed.

Sadly, fear still lurked in her heart, fear that the past might somehow repeat itself. It was an irrational thing, but Chloe couldn't help what she felt, any more than she could change her past.

She stroked his flat stomach and muscular thighs with her palms and fingers. She simultaneously sipped and sucked at his hard flesh. He bucked under her mouth and hands. She teased and she taunted and she seduced, and then she did it again. And again. She persisted until an indescribable sound burst out of Jack.

Chloe didn't deny him when he reached for her, drew her up against his straining body, and rolled her onto her back. He plunged into her a heartbeat later, the moan that followed coming from the depths of his soul. It was a tortured sound, one that Chloe recognized deep in her own heart.

She wrapped her arms around him, offered him her mouth, and circled his hips with her silk-covered legs. He repeatedly drove into her, unable to control the desire raging through him.

She met him thrust for thrust, her body filled to overflowing with his manhood. She succumbed to the tension tightening the insides of her body as she surged up to meet him. She unknowingly scored his back with her fingernails as she clutched at him. Her mouth grew avid as they devoured each other with the kind of hunger that defies both reason and logic.

They climaxed at the same moment, their shocked cries of pleasure mingling, then echoing through the high-ceilinged rooms of the lower floor of the mansion. The force of their blended release overwhelmed them and then hurled them beyond the sensory boundaries of their bodies.

Gasping for air, they clung together as their climaxing bodies spasmed with near violence. The scintillating sensations coursing through them slowly abated, although the aftershocks continued to rumble through their still-joined loins.

They held each other, the warmth of the fireplace allowing them the luxury of remaining unclothed as the clock on the mantel marked the passage of time. After a while they drifted off to sleep, but their hunger for each other eventually wakened them.

Jack and Chloe made love again, but this time with a languid eroticism that proved to be just as devastating to their senses as their first recklessly passionate interlude.

Sometime around midnight they roused themselves from a second nap and shared the last of the cognac.

"You dazzle me, Chloe McNeil," Jack remarked as they sat facing each other on the floor in front of the fire.

Lifting her arms above her head, Chloe stretched. Jack placed his hands over her breasts. Chloe arched into his hands like a lazy feline. He rewarded her by leaning down and lingering at the hard tips, licking and sucking until she trembled beneath his mouth.

She lowered her hands to frame his face. As he fondled the swollen globes he whispered kisses up her chest, over the pulse beating in the hollow of her throat, and across her chin before settling his mouth over hers. He claimed her mouth in a long, lazy kiss.

When he finally drew back from her, Chloe breathlessly remarked, "That dazzling thing is a two-way street, you know. Tonight was wonderful. Just what I needed." Reaching out, she traced the width of his lower lip with her fingertip.

He sucked her finger into his mouth and playfully nibbled on the tip until she laughed and withdrew it. "Can you stand to be dazzled again?"

She gave him an arch look, then scooted closer. "What exactly did you have in mind?"

His own smile fading, Jack searched her features

for a long moment. He took her hands and deliberately laced their fingers together. "Marriage."

Clearly stunned, Chloe stared at Jack.

"I know you aren't in love with me, but we can make it work. I have enough love for both of us."

Tears filled her eyes. "Jack, I . . . you deserve so much more. . . . I don't want to hurt you. . . ." She faltered, her uncertainty evident in her troubled expression and in the tears streaming down her cheeks.

"It's all right, so you don't need to cry. I can deal with the truth, and the truth is that I don't want to live my life without you in it."

"You're serious, aren't you?"

"Extremely." He drew her forward and into his arms. He held her as he spoke quietly. "You don't have to give me an answer right away. Just think about the life we could have together."

"You know my first marriage was a disaster. I'm afraid—"

"You don't ever have to be afraid of me," he cut in. "Not ever, Chloe. I'd rather die than hurt you."

Chloe looped her arms around his shoulders and tucked her damp face into the muscular curve that joined his shoulder to his neck. She started over, her voice shaky as she spoke. "I know that, Jack. It's just that . . ."

He eased free of her encircling arms and shifted her backward so that he could see her face. "Don't make a decision now. It's late, and we're both tired. Just think about what I'm suggesting, think about a life together, the children we could have, and the happiness we could share. Please give the idea some thought, and we'll talk when you're ready."

Chloe reluctantly nodded, then wrapped her arms around him. Her shock slowly gave way to disbelief. Jack loved her enough to ask her to marry him. She'd hoped and prayed for his love, and she was too paralyzed by her past to embrace what he offered. She felt weak and stupid, and incredibly sad.

Jack held her for a very long time. Neither one of them said a word. When the clock in the hallway chimed once, they realized just how late it was. Silently getting to their feet, they dressed, turned out the lights, and left Fairhaven.

Chloe spoke only one more time that night as they stood in the garage at her house. "You really love me?"

The smile he managed was tinged with sadness as he nodded. "So much so that I've had a hard time not saying the words, but I didn't want to scare you away."

She moved into his arms. After a quick hard hug, Jack released her and moved out of reach. "I'll be out in the guest house if you need me during the night. I don't want an answer until you've had time to think. All right?"

Chloe nodded.

Jack caught her arm as she started to turn away. "I'll say good night to Viva and Spence for both of us. Why don't you go ahead to bed after you check on the baby?"

She did as he suggested, promising herself that she would call Viva the next morning and thank her properly for baby-sitting.

Unable to sleep almost an hour later, Chloe stood in the dark beside Matthew's crib. Silent tears streaked her cheeks. She realized that this was the first night that she and Jack had been apart since becoming lovers.

TWELVE

Jack strode into the nursery early the next morning. Clad in jeans, a heavy sweater, and a pair of deck shoes, he looked like a man who'd dressed hurriedly and hadn't taken the time to shave.

Chloe didn't try to hide her surprise at his somewhat disheveled appearance. Seated in the rocking chair, she was feeding the baby his first bottle of the day.

Matthew, eyes wide open as Jack stepped into his field of vision, waved a tiny fist, gurgled his version of a greeting around the nipple in his mouth, and then returned his attention to the contents of his bottle.

Chloe almost smiled at his antics, but a movie of the previous night started playing through her mind. The strained expression on Jack's face was her first clue that something else, aside from their obvious problem, might be wrong. Her anxiety heightened when she noticed the cellular phone gripped in his hand. She resisted believing that it involved Matthew.

"What is it?" she asked, her voice deliberately soft so that she wouldn't alarm the baby.

"Bill just called. He's coming over."

"Now?"

Jack nodded. "He's on his way. He's bringing Matthew's parents with him."

Chloe felt as if someone had plunged a stake into her heart. Badly shaken, she leaned her head against the back of the chair and closed her eyes without disturbing Matthew.

She breathed shallowly, willing herself to stay strong for his sake. A wail of despair echoed in her heart, though. She bit down on her lower lip to keep it from spilling out of her.

"Chloe?"

She opened her eyes to find Jack kneeling beside the rocker. When she felt his hand settle on her shoulder, she exhaled with relief. She knew then that he would do what he always did—he would share his strength as they navigated the troubled waters ahead of them.

"I'm okay," she whispered.

He used his thumb to wipe away the smudge of blood beaded on her lower lip. "Take a deep breath, and then tell me what you want me to do first."

She gave him a blank look. She mentally scrambled for an answer, but it took her a minute to find one. Looking down at Matthew, she realized that he'd dozed off again and that his bottle of formula was empty.

"I need to get dressed. Can you take him for me?"

Jack eased the sleeping infant out of her arms, shifted him into the curve of one strong arm, and then used his free hand to help her get to her feet.

Chloe staggered slightly. Jack caught her against his body. She leaned into his strength, fortifying herself.

"I know you're worried, but try not to expect the worst," Jack urged.

Her chin wobbled, but she nodded. "It's hard," she confessed.

"I know, sweetheart, but we'll get through this for Matthew. He still needs us to do our best."

That reminder strengthened her in ways that nothing else could have. She forced what turned out to be a fragile-looking smile to her lips. "It's not over until it's over," she muttered. She shook her head in disgust at the clichéd remark.

Jack hugged her close with his free arm, then released her. "Something like that."

"I'll be back in a few minutes," she said as she drifted toward the nursery door. She felt directionless, and the feeling unnerved her.

"Take your time," Jack said. "You might feel better if you take a quick shower."

Chloe nodded, glad this one time to be told what to do. She felt too disoriented for clear thought. She headed down the hallway to the master suite, pausing briefly as she passed the bed she'd occupied alone for a few hours that night, then forcing one foot in front of the other until she reached the bathroom.

Chloe jerked the shower fixture to the on position, shed her clothing, and stepped under the needle-sharp spray of ice-cold water. It jarred her back to reality in short order. She knew then that if she didn't want her life going up in flames, she had to do something. Dressed and far more clearheaded twenty minutes later, Chloe hurried out of her bedroom, down the hallway, and into the family room.

"Better?" Jack asked as he handed her a cup of freshly brewed coffee.

"Much better, thank you," she answered, accepting the coffee and taking a sip. She glanced at the bassinet. "He's still asleep?"

"Out like a light, as per usual. He's got his morning drill down to a science."

She smiled around the lip of her cup before taking a second sip of the fragrant brew. "Thank you."

"For what?" he asked as he joined her in front of the French doors. In the distance a fawn and her two spindly-legged newborns nibbled the berries from a clump of shrubs.

She smiled as she peered up at him. "For being you." She studied his angular face. *I love you so much, Jackson Howell, and I haven't even had the courage to tell you. What kind of coward does that make me?*

"Such as I am," he said teasingly as he leaned down and gently touched his lips to hers.

"What you are is pretty unusual," she said. She stiffened in the next moment, because she spotted Bill's patrol car coming up the winding drive. "But I don't think this is the time to go into it."

Jack followed her gaze. "That's Bill, isn't it?"

"Yes." She whispered the word, because she could barely speak. Gripping her cup with both hands, she stared at the advancing vehicle and wished it would disappear. It didn't until it passed behind the barn. In thirty seconds, she knew, Bill and Matthew's parents would pull up in front of the house. In sixty seconds, they'd ring the doorbell.

That was all the time it would take for them to lose Matthew. Her heart lurched painfully in her chest as she reminded herself that he wasn't their child and they couldn't keep him if his parents wanted him back. That was reality, and there was a whole lot of that going around in the world these days. She'd have to adjust. She told herself she could and would adjust.

"You okay?" Jack asked.

She blinked him into focus before she answered. "I'm afraid, but I know we have to do this."

Jack slid his arm around her. "Together, Chloe. We do it together."

She nodded, drawing strength from him once more.

"I love you, Chloe."

His voice rang with certainty and sincerity. Tears filled her eyes, and she longed to say the words back to him.

"I'll get the door," Jack said before he released her and started moving across the family room.

Pausing in the doorway, he glanced back at her before continuing into the hallway. Her smile was tremulous, but it was there for him to see. She knew in that instant that she needed to tell him what was in her heart.

"Jack, I . . ."

He smiled, again offering reassurance. He was always giving, and always caring in little ways that truly counted.

The doorbell rang.

No, she thought. She couldn't believe it. It was too trite, too much of a coincidence.

Jack stepped out of sight just as she said, "I've fallen in love with you, Jack Howell.

"I can say the words again," she reminded herself as she walked over to the bassinet to check on Matthew. "I can think of this as a rehearsal, which I obviously needed since I'm such a darn wuss about trust."

Matthew opened his eyes, kicked his feet, and waved his fists. Chloe smiled at him, leaned down, and gathered him into her arms as Jack led a grim-faced Bill Sturgis and two awkward-looking teen-agers into the family room. When she saw just how young and scared the two were, the stone wall she'd erected around her heart against them crumbled to dust.

"Why don't we all sit down?" Chloe suggested in a kind but confident tone of voice.

She led the way to the couch, patting the cushion beside her as she looked at the young mother. The boy, who was probably all of sixteen, sat beside his girlfriend and gripped her hand. Chloe immediately noticed the awe in their faces as they looked at the beautiful child they'd created.

"Well, folks, I think we got ourselves some serious talkin' to do," began Bill Sturgis. "Bobby, why don't you and Sarah start by telling us why you all decided to leave your boy for Mr. Howell to find at Fairhaven?"

Jack handed Bill a mug of coffee, refreshed his own, and poured glasses of juice for the two teens. His expression somber, he sat down in a chair within reaching distance of Chloe and the baby. Matthew gurgled and blew bubbles.

Almost three hours later Jack and the sheriff walked outside for some fresh air. Because they trusted both her judgment and her instincts, neither man questioned Chloe's request for some time alone with Bobby and Sarah.

A light snow had begun to fall, but they'd dressed for the weather. They strolled along the winding driveway, their heads bowed against the wind and their hands tucked into their jacket pockets to ward off the cold.

"It's hard to believe they managed to keep it from their folks every step of the way, but it sure sounds like they did," the sheriff remarked.

Jack shook his head. "Those two kids redefine scared, don't they? I almost feel sorry for them."

"Leaving the little guy on your porch that way is hard to forgive."

"Very hard," Jack conceded as he glanced at the sheriff. "When I think of the things that could have happened to Matthew, my blood runs cold."

"They're typical kids, and they've made a whole string of dumb mistakes, but maybe they're about to do something smart. I sure hope so."

Jack nodded at Bill as they walked along the driveway. "Whatever they decide to do, I'm going to petition the court for guardianship of Matthew. I don't want him to fall through the legal cracks if they panic again. Will you back me up?" he asked.

"Of course, but what about Chloe?"

"What about her?" he replied, painfully aware of the fact that the woman he loved didn't return his feelings. Although he hoped that they would share the future, he counseled himself not to count on it. Only Chloe knew if she would be able to move beyond her past.

"I thought you two were pretty serious. In fact, I kind of expected . . ." He paused and cleared his throat. "Well, you know what I mean."

Jack came to a stop and faced the sheriff. He saw the curiosity in the man's weathered features, and he couldn't fault him for wondering. "I'd like to think that things will work out between us, but if they don't, I'm not taking any chances with Matthew's welfare. He's a separate issue at this point."

"I'll take your word for it," Bill said, looking more than a little confused.

"I've asked Chloe to marry me, but she hasn't given me an answer yet. She may need some time. More time than Matthew might have if the court steps in and custody becomes an issue."

"Her past worries her, I suspect, even though it's obvious you aren't anything like Marty." When Jack didn't respond right away, Bill resumed walking.

Jack fell into step beside the sheriff. He finally admitted, "I've come to the same conclusion, although I have to confess that I'm getting awfully tired of dealing with the ghost of a dead man. Especially since he was such a bastard to her."

"Be patient with Chloe. She went through hell because of that sorry son of a gun. Everyone in town thinks it's a small miracle that she's even managed to rebuild her life."

"I'm trying to be patient, but whatever happens," Jack cautioned his new friend, "I intend to protect Matthew."

"I'd expect that of you, especially since I know how much you care about the boy."

Conversation between them waned as the snowfall intensified and the wind gusts gained strength. The two men eventually reversed course and headed back in the direction of the house.

Once they'd entered the house and secured the front door, they put their coats in the hall closet. As they made their way to the family room they heard voices filled with laughter.

Jack thought it was a nice change of pace from the tears and recriminations of the last few hours, although he wondered what was causing it. He paused in the doorway, his answer in the bassinet on the far side of the room.

Jack was pleased that Chloe had encouraged Sarah and Bobby to become better acquainted with Matthew. For his part, the baby waved his arms and kicked his little legs with abandon while he gurgled and cooed.

"Looks like everyone's had a chance to relax," Jack observed as he strolled toward Chloe. When she met his gaze and smiled at him, he saw that her fear and panic had abated. He slid his arm around her shoulders and hugged her close.

Bobby Munroe made his way to the center of the room, a look of uncertainty on his youthful face. Sarah followed along and stood just behind him.

Jack waited while the teen nervously rubbed the palms of his hands against his thighs, then took another step closer. Sarah edged a step forward as well.

"Mr. Howell, sir, Sarah and I want to apologize for what we've done, and we want to thank you. We knew about you from talk in town, and one of the things we'd heard was that you didn't grow up with your daddy because you-all didn't know about each other. We figured you'd understand about Matthew, and we hoped you'd want to look out for him. We know we can't take proper care of him, so we're asking you to help us help him. We want what's best for him, sir. We really do," he finished earnestly.

Jack gave himself a moment to consider his reply. Despite the poor judgment the two had displayed, the last thing he wanted to do was destroy the fledgling confidence of a boy who had been forced to become a man in a big hurry.

"I accept your apology, Bobby, but I want your promise that you'll be man enough to tell Matthew the truth of what you did and why. You owe him that much when he's old enough to understand. In the end, his forgiveness is far more important than mine."

The young man nodded. "I know you're right, sir, and I'll make you that promise."

Sarah stopped hiding behind Bobby. Once she moved into view she clasped his hand and spoke for them both. "We're giving him up for adoption, Mr. Howell. We've decided that's the best thing to do for Matthew. Miss Chloe said it was a decision we needed to make on our own, so we talked, just the two of us, and we decided. Since you're a lawyer, will you help us find a good family for Matthew?"

Jack met Chloe's gaze. He saw the uncertainty in her features. He thought then about the question he'd asked her the night before. The question she hadn't answered yet. The question she might never answer.

"Mr. Howell?" Sarah said.

Bill filled in the ensuing silence. "I think we're getting a little ahead of ourselves here."

Sarah sidled up against Bobby, an anxious look on her face. "I don't understand."

The teenage boy on the verge of manhood slipped his arm around his girl and squared his narrow shoulders. "Me neither, Sheriff."

"Your folks? Don't you think you need to talk to them before you do anything else?"

"They'll kill us," Sarah said. Sagging against Bobby, she paled. "We can't tell them, not alone. Please don't make us."

"Sheriff?" Bobby squeaked. He swallowed nervously and got his voice under control. "Sheriff, we're gonna need help explaining things to them. We're in way over our heads. We were stupid, and we know it. Even though we tried to make things right, we still made a mess of it all."

Bill shook his head, his willingness to take pity on the teenagers apparent as he dealt with their concern. "I'll speak to them with you, but it's not exactly the kind of Christmas gift they'll be expecting. In fact, the Munroes and the Rayburns are going to be none too pleased." He exhaled, the gust of air a noisy punctuation mark on his comments. "In the meantime I think Jack and Chloe should maintain custody of the little fella. He's happy and well cared for here, and you won't have to worry about him."

Bobby and Sarah nodded vigorously.

Jack nearly smiled. Two innocents had given birth to another innocent. They all needed to be protected and loved. He wondered if he was getting soft, or old, or both. He stopped wondering, though, when Chloe turned to look up at him. He studied her, but her expression didn't prepare him for her next remark.

"Jack and I are engaged to be married."

Everyone in the room, including Jack, stared at her. The shock resonating inside him made him wonder if he was hearing things.

Chloe met the stunned gaze of the man she loved. "If he still wants to marry me, and if he's not totally fed up with the shrinking violet routine I've been doing lately." When he said nothing, she took a steadying breath. "Aren't we?" she asked. "Engaged, I mean."

Jack snapped out of his shock in short order. "We're engaged," he confirmed, drawing her close. At that moment he didn't care why she'd made the decision. The fact that she had was enough.

"Outstanding!" Bill exclaimed as he grasped Jack's free hand and pumped it up and down.

"And we're interested in starting a family," Chloe said, not missing a beat.

Jack nodded, although he felt somewhat poleaxed by the unconventional manner in which Chloe had accepted his proposal. "That's also true."

"You'd be perfect for Matthew!" Sarah exclaimed. "If I could pick his momma for him, I'd pick you, Miss Chloe."

She smiled at the girl. "We love him, Sarah, and we'd give him a good home."

"Would we be able to visit him?" Bobby asked quietly.

Good for you, Jack thought as he studied the boy.

There's hope for you yet. Jack's past further strengthened his perspective on what was best for everyone
involved, especially the baby. "Matthew has a right
to know his birth parents. If we adopt him, we'd
expect you both to be a part of his life."

"I agree," Chloe said, clearly committed to giving Matthew the very best. "Matthew should know
the truth about his origins."

Tears flooded Bobby's eyes. The teenager struggled not to fall apart in front of Sarah and the three
adults in the room. When he'd finally regained control of himself, he said, "Thank you, sir. Thank you,
ma'am."

"You're very welcome," Jack said, some of the
tension of the last days and weeks starting to dissi-
pate.

He knew they faced a tedious process in the
courts, not to mention a mountain of paperwork
once they secured the cooperation of Bobby's and
Sarah's families, but he considered Matthew's welfare far more important than the potential hassles
ahead of them.

What he suddenly couldn't quite come to terms
with was Chloe's change of heart, although he refrained from saying anything. She'd accepted his
marriage proposal. Did she love him at all? Or was
Matthew the only reason she'd agreed to marry him?
he wondered.

Hard questions, but questions that needed answers, nonetheless. Jack knew himself well enough
to realize that he wouldn't know any peace until he

heard the truth from Chloe. This was not the time, though. Later, when they had time alone, they would talk, he promised himself.

"Congratulations, you two," Bill said, shaking hands with Jack and hugging Chloe before he turned to Bobby and Sarah. "Why don't we get through the Christmas holidays, and then we'll have us a meeting with all the families?"

"With one proviso," Jack added.

Bill smiled broadly. "You sounded like Tommy just then, so I'm definitely listening."

"Let's get these two in front of Lisa Hampton as soon as possible. We all trust her, and she knows the Social Services system better than any of us. She's Matthew's advocate as far as the court is concerned, so it makes sense to have her in the proverbial loop."

Chloe glanced at her watch. "She probably hasn't left for lunch yet, so why don't I call her and ask her to join us here?"

"Let me make the call," Bill offered, shepherding Sarah and Bobby out of the family room in short order. "You two take a little break, why don't you?"

As Bill and the teenagers disappeared down the hallway Jack tugged Chloe into his arms and held her. "You surprised me," he admitted as he ran his hands up and down her back.

Smiling, she looked up at him. "I thought I might have. Did you mind terribly?"

He shook his head. "I didn't mind at all." He hesitated.

"But?" Chloe prompted.

Jack shrugged, but the gesture failed to ease the worry lingering in his hazel eyes.

"There's something you're not saying." She pressed a kiss to his chin, then waited for him to speak.

"Tonight's Christmas Eve," he remarked.

Confused, Chloe frowned. "What's that got to do with anything?"

"I've already received two of the three things I wanted for Christmas," he mused.

She smiled. "Tell me more."

He cocked his head to one side, as though considering her request.

"You don't want to spoil the surprise?" she speculated when he didn't say anything.

"Let's deal with it tonight," he suggested. "We've got a lot going on right now, and this isn't a good time to talk."

"Jack . . ." she began.

He silenced her with his lips as he leaned down and claimed her mouth in a burst of hunger. His passion for her flared as he explored her mouth, his tongue a scavenger as he satisfied his need for her.

Chloe sank into him and into his kiss. She surrendered completely to Jack, losing track of everything but him. As her body started to ache with escalating desire, she remembered that there were other people in the house.

When Chloe sagged in his arms, Jack relinquished her lips. Peering up at him, she saw how dark his eyes had become and felt his hands skimming up under the hem of her sweater. "You're kill-ing me." She groaned softly.

He shuddered, captivated by the feel of her silky skin beneath his fingers and palms and tantalized by the erotic sound of her voice. Shifting his hands, he used them like brackets and aligned their hips. He let her feel the strength of his hunger for her as he nudged against her. Moaning, she squirmed even closer and rocked her pelvis against his.

Jack gave her a pained look. "Careful."

"We're not alone," she breathlessly reminded him.

"We aren't, are we?" he clarified somewhat wryly.

Chloe shook her head.

"But we will be tonight. Why don't we spend it at Fairhaven?"

She smiled. "You've got yourself a deal, Mr. Howell," she said just as Matthew started to fuss.

"Long day," Chloe said once she'd settled a sleeping Matthew into his travel basket and pulled the blanket up to his shoulders. Turning, she glanced at Jack as he walked toward her. "Eventful day."

"You have a gift for understatement," he told her as he took her by the hand and led her across the room to a spot in front of the Christmas tree. Reaching for a small beribboned box he'd left on a table next to the tree, he placed it in the palm of her hand.

"What's this?" Chloe asked.

"Something I thought you might like. Why don't you open it and tell me what you think of it?"

Chloe studied the tiny package and then looked up at Jack. "I thought we were going to open our gifts on Christmas morning."

He leaned down and kissed the tip of her nose. "This is one present that can't be delayed, so why don't you humor me."

She inspected it with care. "Is it perishable?"

Jack grinned at her. "Doubtful."

"It's too small to be a fruitcake."

"True."

"I think I'll wait," she teased. "After all, anticipation is part of the fun of Christmas."

He caught her as she tried to bend down and put the package under the tree. "No, Ms. McNeil, you will not wait, but there is a question I need answered first."

Straightening, she gave him a quizzical look. He sounded very serious.

"Why did you change your mind today, Chloe?"

Chloe smiled, glad finally to be able to speak from her heart. "It was the right thing to do," she said softly.

"For Matthew?"

She shook her head. "For all of us."

"And?" he said.

She saw the vulnerability in his angular features, heard it in the tone of his voice. She suddenly realized that Jack didn't have a clue about the depth of her feelings for him. Reaching up, she looped her arms around his neck. "You don't know, do you?"

"Know what, Chloe?" he asked, a hint of wariness in his voice.

"That I'm in love with you. I have been from the start, I think, but I was afraid to tell you until today. I needed to be sure that I wouldn't turn tail and run if we had problems."

"And you're sure now?" he clarified.

"I'm very sure. I tried to tell you before Bill arrived with Bobby and Sarah, but by the time I got up the nerve, the doorbell rang and you went to answer it. Things got a little crazy after that, and this is the first quiet moment we've had all day."

He gathered her into his arms, holding her as though she were the most fragile thing in the world. "Are you really sure, Chloe?"

"I wouldn't marry you if I hadn't looks like fallen in love with you, Jack. We both deserve to be loved for ourselves, and not for any other reason. Marriage for Matthew's sake would be wrong."

He kissed her then, kissed her with such gentleness that she nearly wept. She said a silent prayer of thanks for both Jack and Matthew. She knew in her heart that they would have a good life together, and it would be based on the love and trust that comes from weathering painful times.

Once he released her lips and lifted his head, he said, "I love you, Chloe. I always will. And I promise you that the past is over. You'll never have to revisit it again."

"I believe you," she whispered, tears in her eyes as she gazed up at him.

"Open your present," he urged.

"Bossy man," she chided with a laugh.

"Just this once," he told her.

"All right." Chloe opened the tiny package, carefully peeling back the flocked velvet paper and delicate ribbon used to wrap it. She glanced up at Jack as she held the tiny container. "Now?"

"Please," he said quietly.

She opened the box, her eyes widening with shock and delight when she saw the wide diamond-encrusted band. "Oh, my," she said with awe. "It's gorgeous."

"You like it?"

She met his gaze. "Like is much too tame a word for what this ring represents."

He removed the ring and set aside the box. "Will you share your life with me, Chloe McNeil? Will you be my partner in all things? Will you make my dreams come true?" he asked as he slipped the ring onto her finger.

Tears flooded her eyes. "I will share my life with you, Jackson Howell. I will be your partner in all things. And, together, we'll make all our dreams come true," she promised.

"My dreams have come true. You, your love, and Matthew are my gifts," he told her as he held her to his heart.

"We are?" Chloe whispered, knowing that he spoke the truth as she gazed into his eyes and feeling overwhelmed by the emotions coursing through her because of this unique man.

He gently kissed her, then smiled down at her. "You are. I've never received anything more precious than your love and the family we've begun with Matthew. I've never wanted anything more than what I've found with you."

"I love you, Jack. So much more than I ever thought I'd be able to love anyone."

He smiled and lowered his head once more to claim Chloe's lips in a kiss that sealed the promise of a shared love and a shared future.

THE EDITORS' CORNER

The new year is once again upon us, and we're ushering it in with four new LOVESWEPTs to grace your bookshelves. From the mountains of Kentucky and Nevada to the beaches of Florida, we'll take you to places only your heart can go! So curl up in a comfy chair and hide out from the rest of the world while you plan a christening party with Peggy, catch a killer with Ruth, rescue a pirate with Cynthia, and camp out in the Sierras with Jill.

First is **ANGELS ON ZEBRAS,** LOVESWEPT #866, by the well-loved Peggy Webb. Attorney Joseph Patrick Beauregard refuses to allow Maxie Corban to include zebras at their godson's christening party. Inappropriate, he says. And that's just the beginning! Joe likes his orderly life just fine, and Maxie can't help but try to shake it up by playing the brazen hussy to Joe's conservative legal eagle. Suffice it to say, a steamy yet tenuous relationship ensues, as they learn they can't keep their hands off each other! You may remember Joe and Maxie's relatives as B. J. Corban and Crash Beauregard from BRINGING UP BAXTER, LOVESWEPT #847. Peggy Webb stuns us with another sensual tale of love and laughter in this enchanting mix of sizzle and whimsy.

Ex-cop Rafe Ramirez has no choice but to become the hero of a little girl determined to save her mom in Ruth Owen's **SOMEONE TO WATCH OVER ME**, LOVESWEPT #867. TV anchorwoman Tory Chandler has been receiving dangerous riddles and rhymes written in bloodred ink. Knowing her past is about to rear its ugly head, she wants nothing more than to ignore the threats that have her on edge. Rafe can't ignore them, however, since he's given Tory's daughter his word. Protecting the beautiful temptress who so openly betrayed him is the hardest assignment he's ever had to face. Now that he's back on the road to recovery, can this compassionate warrior keep Tory safe from her worst nightmares? LOVESWEPT favorite Ruth Owen explores the healing of two wounded souls in this story of dark emotions and desperate yearnings.

In **YOUR PLACE OR MINE?**, LOVESWEPT #868, by Cynthia Powell, Captain Diego Swift wakes to find himself stranded in a time much different from his own, and becomes engaged in an argument with the demure she-devil who has besieged his home. Catalina Steadwell had prayed for help from above, though admittedly this half-drowned, naked sailor was not what she was expecting. Though Cat doesn't believe this man's ravings about the nineteenth century, she does need a man around her dilapidated house, and hires Diego as her handyman. After all, the job market for pirates has pretty much dwindled to nothing. When Diego becomes involved in a local gang war, he learns to make use of his second chance at life and love. Here's a positively scrumptious tale by Cynthia Powell that's sure to fulfill every woman's dream of a seafaring, swashbuckling hero!

In **SHOW ME THE WAY**, LOVESWEPT #869, by Jill Shalvis, Katherine Wilson ventures into the wilds of the high Sierras in a desperate attempt to stay alive. Outfitter Kyle Spencer challenges the pretty prosecutor to accompany his group in conquering the elements, but Katy is a city girl at heart. As danger stalks them through God's country, suddenly nothing in the woods is as innocent as it seems. Kyle knows that something is terrifying Katy and wants desperately to help her, but how can he when the woman won't let him near her? Their attraction grows as their time together ebbs, and soon Katy will have to make a choice. Will she entrust Kyle with her life and her heart, or will the maniac who's after her succeed in destroying her? In this journey of survival and discovery, Jill Shalvis shows us once again how believing in love can save you from yourself.

Happy reading!

With warmest wishes,

Susann Brailey

Joy Abella

Susann Brailey   Joy Abella

Senior Editor   Administrative Editor

P.S. Look for these Bantam women's fiction titles coming in January! National bestseller Patricia Potter delivers **STARCATCHER.** On the eve before Lady Marsali Mackey's wedding, she is kidnapped by Patrick Sutherland, Earl of Trydan, and the man who had promised to marry her twelve years ago. And Lisa Gardner, who may be familiar as Silhouette author Alicia Scott, makes her chilling suspense debut with **THE PERFECT HUSBAND,** a novel about a woman who teams up with a mercenary to catch a serial killer. And immediately following this page, preview the Bantam women's fiction titles on sale in November!

For current information on Bantam's women's fiction, visit our new Web site, *Isn't It Romantic*, at the following address:

http://www.bdd.com/romance

Don't miss these extraordinary books
from your favorite Bantam authors!

On sale in November:

TIDINGS OF GREAT JOY
by Sandra Brown

LONG AFTER MIDNIGHT
by Iris Johansen

TABOO
by Susan Johnson

STOLEN MOMENTS
by Michelle Martin

Now in paperback!

LONG AFTER MIDNIGHT

by *New York Times* bestselling author

Iris Johansen

*The first warning was triggered hundreds of miles away.
The second warning exploded only yards from where she
and her son stood. Now Kate Denby realizes the frightening truth: She is somebody's target.*

*Danger has arrived in Kate's backyard with a vengeance.
And the gifted scientist is awakening to a nightmare world
where a ruthless killer is stalking her . . . where her innocent son is considered expendable . . . and where the
medical research to which she has devoted her life is the
same research that could get her killed. Her only hope of
protecting her family and making that medical break-
through is to elude her enemy until she can face him on her
own ground, on her own terms—and destroy him.*

Joshua remained awake for almost an hour, and
even after his eyes finally closed, he slept fitfully.

It was just as well they were going away, Kate
thought. Joshua wasn't a high-strung child, but what
he'd gone through was enough to unsettle anyone.

Phyliss's door was closed, Kate noted when she
reached the hall. She should probably get to bed too.
Not that she'd be able to sleep. She hadn't lied to
Joshua; she was nervous and uneasy . . . and bitterly

resentful. This was her home, it was supposed to be a haven. She didn't like to think of it as a fortress.

But, like it or not, it was a fortress at the moment and she'd better make sure the soldiers were on the battlements. She checked the lock on the front door before she moved quickly toward the living room. She would see the black-and-white from the picture window.

Phyliss, as usual, had drawn the drapes over the window before she went to bed. The cave instinct, Kate thought as she reached for the cord. Close out the outside world and make your own. She and Phyliss were in complete agree—

He was standing outside the window, so close they were separated only by a quarter of an inch of glass.

Oh God. High concave cheekbones, long black straight hair drawn back in a queue, beaded necklace. It was him . . . Ishmaru.

And he was smiling at her.

His lips moved and he was so near she could hear the words through the glass. "You weren't supposed to see me before I got in, Kate." He held her gaze as he showed her the glass cutter in his hand. "But it's all right. I'm almost finished and I like it better this way."

She couldn't move. She stared at him, mesmerized.

"You might as well let me in. You can't stop me."

She jerked the drapes shut, closing him out.

Barricading herself inside with only a fragment of glass, a scrap of material . . .

She heard the sound of blade on glass.

She backed away from the window, stumbled on the hassock, almost fell, righted herself.

Oh God. Where was that policeman? The porch light was out, but surely he could see Ishmaru.

Maybe the policeman wasn't there.

And your husband never mentioned bribery in the ranks?

The drapes were moving.

He'd cut the window.

"Phyliss!" She ran down the hall. "Wake up." She threw open Joshua's door, flew across the room, and jerked him out of bed.

"Mom?"

"Shh, be very quiet. Just do what I tell you, okay?"

"What's wrong?" Phyliss was standing in the doorway. "Is Joshua sick?"

"I want you to leave here." She pushed Joshua toward her. "There's someone outside." She hoped he was still outside. Christ, he could be in the living room by now. "I want you to take Joshua out the back door and over to the Brocklemans'."

Phyliss instantly took Joshua's hand and moved toward the kitchen door. "What about you?"

She heard a sound in the living room. "*Go.* I'll be right behind you."

Phyliss and Joshua flew out the back door.

"Are you waiting for me, Kate?"

He sounded so close, too close. Phyliss and Joshua could not have reached the fence yet. No time to run. Stop him.

She saw him, a shadow in the doorway leading to the hall.

Where was the gun?

In her handbag on the living room table. She couldn't get past him. She backed toward the stove.

Phyliss usually left a frying pan out to cook breakfast in the morning. . . .

"I told you I was coming in. No one can stop me tonight. I had a sign."

She didn't see a weapon but the darkness was lit only by moonlight streaming through the window.

"Give up, Kate."

Her hand closed on the handle of the frying pan. "Leave me *alone*." She leaped forward and struck out at his head with all her strength.

He moved too fast but she connected with a glancing blow.

He was falling. . . .

She streaked past him down the hall. Get to the purse, the gun.

She heard him behind her.

She snatched up the handbag, lunged for the door, and threw the bolt.

Get to the policeman in the black-and-white.

She fumbled with the catch on her purse as she streaked down the driveway toward the black-and-white. Her hand closed on the gun and she threw the purse aside.

"He's not there, Kate," Ishmaru said behind her. "It's just the two of us."

"Susan Johnson's love scenes sparkle, sizzle, and burn!"   —*Affaire de Coeur*

Through eleven nationally bestselling books, award winner Susan Johnson has won a legion of fans for her lushly romantic historical novels. Now she delivers her most thrilling tale yet—a searing blend of rousing adventure and wild, forbidden love . . .

TABOO

by Susan Johnson

Married against her will to the brutal Russian general who conquered her people, Countess Teo Korsakova has never known what it means to want a man . . . until now. Trapped behind enemy lines, held captive by her husband's most formidable foe, she should fear for her life. But all Teo feels in General Andre Duras's shattering presence is breathless passion. France's most victorious commander, Andre knows that he should do the honorable thing, knows too that on the eve of battle he cannot afford so luscious a distraction. Yet something about Teo lures him to do the unthinkable: to seduce his enemy's wife, and to let himself love a woman who can never be his.

He played chess the way he approached warfare, moving quickly, decisively, always on the attack. But she held her own, although her style was less aggressive, and when he took her first knight after long contention for its position, he said, "If your husband's half as good as you, he'll be a formidable opponent."

"I'm not sure you fight the same way."

"You've seen him in battle?"

"On a small scale. Against my grandfather in Siberia."

"And yet you married him?"

"Not by choice. The Russians traditionally take hostages from their conquered tribes. I'm the Siberian version. My clan sends my husband tribute in gold each year. So you see why I'm valuable to him."

"Not for gold alone, I'm sure," he said, beginning to move his rook.

"How gallant, Andre," she playfully declared.

His gaze came up at the sound of his name, his rook poised over the board, and their glances held for a moment. The fire crackled noisily in the hearth, the ticking of the clock sounded loud in the stillness, the air suddenly took on a charged hush, and then the general smiled—a smooth, charming smile. "You're going to lose your bishop, Teo."

She couldn't answer as suavely because her breath was caught in her throat and it took her a second to overcome the strange, heated feeling inundating her senses.

His gaze slid down her blushing cheeks and throat to rest briefly on her taut nipples visible through her white cashmere robe and he wondered what was happening to him that so demure a sight had such a staggering effect on his libido. He dropped his rook precipitously into place, inhaled, and leaned back in his chair, as if putting distance between himself and such tremulous innocence would suffice to restore his reason.

"Your move," he gruffly said.

"Maybe we shouldn't play anymore."

"Your move." It was his soft voice of command.

"I don't take orders."

"I'd appreciate it if you'd move."

"I'm not sure I know what I'm doing anymore." He lounged across from her, tall, lean, powerful, with predatory eyes, the softest of voices, and the capacity to make her tremble.

"It's only a game."

"This, you mean."

"Of course. What else would I mean?"

"I was married when I was fifteen, after two years of refinement at the Smolny Institute for Noble Girls," she pertinently said, wanting him to know.

"And you're very refined," he urbanely replied, wondering how much she knew of love after thirteen faithful years in a forced marriage. His eyes drifted downward again, his thoughts no longer of chess.

"My husband's not refined at all."

"Many Russians aren't." He could feel his erection begin to rise, the thought of showing her another side of passionate desire ruinous to his self-restraint.

"It's getting late," she murmured, her voice quavering slightly.

"I'll see you upstairs," he softly said.

When he stood, his desire was obvious; the form-fitting regimentals molded his body like a second skin.

Gripping the chair arms, she said, "No," her voice no more than a whisper.

He moved around the small table and touched her then because he couldn't help himself, because she was quivering with desire like some virginal young girl and the intoxicating image of such tremulous need was more carnal than anything he'd ever experienced. His hand fell lightly on her shoulder, its heat tantalizing, tempting.

She looked up at him and, lifting her mouth to his, heard herself say, "Kiss me."

"Take my hand," he murmured. And when she did, he pulled her to her feet and drew her close so the scent of her was in his nostrils and the warmth of her body touched his.

"Give me a child." Some inner voice prompted the words she'd only dreamed for years.

"No," he calmly said, as if she hadn't asked the unthinkable from a stranger, and then his mouth covered hers and she sighed against his lips. And as their kiss deepened and heated their blood and drove away reason, they both felt an indefinable bliss—torrid and languorous, heartfelt and, most strangely—hopeful in two people who had long ago become disenchanted with hope.

And then her maid's voice drifted down the stairway, the intonation of her native tongue without inflection. "He'll kill you," she declared.

Duras's mouth lifted and his head turned to the sound. "What did she say?"

"She reminded me of the consequences."

"Which are?"

"My husband's wrath."

He was a hairsbreadth from selfishly saying, *Don't worry*, but her body had gone rigid in his arms at her maid's pointed admonition and at base he knew better. He knew he wouldn't be there to protect her from her husband's anger and he knew too that she was much too innocent for a casual night of love.

"Tamyr is my voice of reason."

He released her and took a step away, as if he couldn't trust himself to so benignly relinquish such powerful feeling. "We all need a voice of reason," he neutrally said. "Thank you for the game of chess."

"I'm sorry."

"Not more sorry than I," Duras said with a brief smile.

"Will I see you again?" She couldn't help herself from asking.

"Certainly." He took another step back, his need for her almost overwhelming. "And if you wish for anything during your stay with us, feel free to call on Bonnay."

"Can't I call on you?"

"My schedule's frenzied and, more precisely, your maid's voice may not be able to curtail me a second time."

"I see."

"Forgive my bluntness."

"Forgiven," she gently said.

"Good night, Madame Countess." He bowed with grace.

"Good night, Andre."

"Under other circumstances . . ." he began, and then shrugged away useless explanation.

"I know," she softly said. "Thank you."

He left precipitously, retreat uncommon for France's bravest general, but he wasn't sure he could trust himself to act the gentleman if he stayed.

"Michelle Martin writes fresh, funny, fast-paced contemporary romance with a delicious hint of suspense."
—Teresa Medeiros, nationally bestselling author of *Touch of Enchantment*

The irresistible Michelle Martin, author of *Stolen Hearts*, whips up a delectable new concoction of a woman chasing a dream . . . and the man who fulfills her sweetest fantasies . . .

STOLEN MOMENTS

by Michelle Martin

It was just after midnight when the Princess of Pop made her escape, leaving behind the syrupy-sweet ballads and the tyrannical manager who had made her famous. All Harley Jane Miller wanted was a vacation: two weeks on her own in New York before recording her next album. Yet now that she's tasted freedom, the Princess of Pop's gone electric: changing her clothes, her music, and her good-girl image. And she's never going back. Harley knows it will take some quick thinking to shake her greedy manager. But she never suspects she'll be waylaid by a diamond heist, the French mafia, and *a devastatingly gorgeous detective who's determined to bring her in—by way of his bedroom . . . and when he does, Harley Jane will be more than willing to comply . . .*

"Hello again, Miss Miller."
    Harley's heart stopped. There was a roaring in her

ears. Slowly she turned her head and looked up. A man stood beside her bench. It was the hunk from Manny's, and he knew who she was. Staring up into those dark eyes, she knew it was futile for her to even attempt to pretend that she didn't know that he knew who she was. "Are you Duncan Lang, the man who was asking questions about me at the RIHGA yesterday?"

"One and the same."

"Did Boyd send you?"

"Boyd *hired* me. I found you thanks to high technology and brilliant deductive reasoning."

Harley stared up at him. "Can you be bought off?"

His dark eyes crinkled in amusement. " 'Fraid not. Dad would be peeved. Colangco has a sterling reputation for honesty and results. Sorry," he said as he picked up her Maxi-Mouse. "Shall we head back to the Hilton for your things?"

Crud, he knew where she was staying. Harley tried to think, but her brain felt like iced sludge. It was over. She hadn't even had two full days of freedom yet, and it was over.

Her chest ached. "I'm twenty-six, a grown woman, legally independent," she stated. "You can't just haul me back to Boyd like he *owns* me!"

"I can when that's what I'm hired to do."

"But I haven't even had a chance to try out my new guitar," Harley said, hot tears welling in her eyes. She hurriedly pushed them back. "Boyd is not about to let me keep it. He hates electric guitars. He doesn't think they're feminine."

"What?"

"And he won't let me wear black clothes, or red

clothes, or anything resembling a bright color. And no jeans. Not even slacks."

"He's got a tight rein on you," Duncan Lang agreed as he sat down beside her.

"He is sucking the life's blood out of me."

"Why do you let him?"

"Boyd is deaf to anyone's 'no' except his own," Harley replied bitterly.

"But as you pointed out, you are twenty-six and legally independent. You don't have to put up with his crap if you don't want to."

"Why do you care?" Harley demanded, glaring up at the treacherous hunk.

"I don't," Duncan Lang stated. "I'm just curious. You did a very good job of hiding yourself among eight million people—"

"*You* found me."

"Ah, well," he said, ducking his head in false modesty, "I'm a trained investigator, after all." His winsome smile must have charmed every female who'd even glanced at him sideways from the time he was sixteen. It made Harley's teeth grate. "My point is that," he continued, "Boyd's opinion notwithstanding, you seem fully capable of taking care of yourself. Fire the control freak and get on with your life."

"It's not that easy," Harley said, her arms tightening around the guitar case. "I owe everything to Boyd: my career, my success, my fame, my money. I'd still be a little hick from Oklahoma if it weren't for him. And I'm not so sure I can make it in the industry without him now."

"He *has* run a number on you, hasn't he?"

"Oh yeah," Harley said, staring down at the concrete ground.

"So why did you run away?"

Harley felt her stomach freeze over. Her jaws began to liquefy. She stared blindly at the fountain. "The music stopped coming," she whispered.

"I thought so," Duncan Lang said.

Harley turned her head and met his sympathetic black gaze. It nearly undid her. Oh God, her music! "It's been two months and not a note, not a lyric." The well she had depended on all of her life had gone dry. There was nothing left to be tapped. She looked up at him, pleading for a stay of execution. "I thought if I could just have a few weeks of fun. A few weeks of not being Jane Miller. A few weeks of just letting go, and maybe it would come back. Maybe I'd be okay again. Then I'd fly to L.A., get back on the treadmill, and make the damn album for Sony."

Harley almost clapped a hand to her mouth. Years ago Boyd had forbidden Jane Miller to swear in public or private.

"A reasonable plan," Lang agreed.

"Then let me go!" Harley said, her hand clutching his arm. "Let me have my two weeks. No one will be hurt. I'll come back and fulfill all of my obligations, I promise."

"Sorry, Princess, that's not part of the plan."

"Who the *hell* do you think you are?" Harley exploded. "You're not God. You have no right to tell me where to go or what to do. I'll fly off to *Brazil* if I feel like it and you can't stop me."

"Oh yes I can," he retorted.

"How?"

"By physical force if necessary."

He looked like he could do it too. "*Oh*, I hate men," Harley seethed. "The arrogance. The stupidity."

"I'm actually pretty intelligent," Duncan Lang retorted, dark eyes glittering. "Don't forget, I found you."

"If you found me, you can lose me."

"No."

"Dammit, Lang—"

"I signed a contract, Princess. I am obligated to fulfill it."

"But not today," Harley pleaded. "You don't have to fulfill it today, or tomorrow, or even a week from tomorrow. Give me back my holiday, Mr. Lang."

He looked down at her. A gamine with breasts, dressed all in black. He'd known an odd kind of fascination as he'd surreptitiously watched her in Manny's Music. She had a quality . . . like Sleeping Beauty just waking up from a hundred years' sleep and discovering the world anew.

He'd never felt that kind of immediate attraction to a woman in his life. Oh sure, he'd been drawn to beautiful women, and voluptuous women, and even bewitching women. Harley was none of those things. She was just somehow . . . familiar.

"Okay, Princess, here's the deal," he said with sudden decision. "I'll do a little digging while you make like a tourist or a musician or whatever the hell it is you want to be today. But at midnight I put you back in your pumpkin and return you to Mr. Monroe." Duncan held out his hand. "Deal?"

Faux brown eyes stared up at him a moment. Then Harley Jane Miller's slim fingers slid across his hand, clasping it firmly, disconcerting him with a sudden feeling of connection. "Deal."

DON'T MISS THESE FABULOUS
BANTAM WOMEN'S FICTION TITLES